T5-COB-456

The Hands of Eddy Loyd

Other books by E. Richard Johnson
Blind Man's Bluff
Silver Street

THE HANDS OF EDDY LOYD

E. RICHARD JOHNSON

A Joan Kahn Book

ST. MARTIN'S PRESS
NEW YORK

THE HANDS OF EDDY LOYD. Copyright © 1988 by E. Richard Johnson. All rights reserved. Printed in the United States of America. No part of this book may be used or reproduced in any manner whatsoever without written permission except in the case of brief quotations embodied in critical articles or reviews. For information, address St. Martin's Press, 175 Fifth Avenue, New York, N.Y. 10010.

Library of Congress Cataloging-in-Publication Data

Johnson, E. Richard, 1937–
   The hands of Eddy Loyd / by E. Richard Johnson
     p. cm.
   ISBN 0-312-01771-5
   I. Title.
PS3560.O376H3 1988
813'.54—dc19   87-38251

"A Joan Kahn Book"

First Edition

10 9 8 7 6 5 4 3 2 1

This one is for Mom and Dad

1

Fall.

It was the best time of the year in the city for some. A time of cool nights and bright, warm days between the humid, baking heat of summer and the ice-locked grip of winter when icy storms could bring the city to a silent, shivering halt.

In the park on Rice Street you could walk through the yellow and red shades of frost-touched trees or watch the kids build careful piles of fallen leaves for the single purpose of one brief dive through them. You could stare at the brownstones across from the park in wonder because in the warm sun they could appear softly colored and dignified, overlooking the park and the distant river that sometimes seemed blue this time of the year.

In the distance to the south, the clear fingers of the new city reached up into the sky in a broken pattern as if someone could not decide which shape would best serve and had instead tested towers, spheres, rectangles, and octagons with domes. There was even a tall glass tower with a mushroom cap thrust up against the clear blue sky.

If you were foolish enough to be anywhere near the park after dark, you could view a brightly lit city skyline against a web of stars. Even during the day, with a clear eye you could see that the dignified brownstones were shabby from years of neglect and most of the windows overlooking the park were missing or replaced with cardboard. And if the wind shifted you could receive the ripe odor of the stockyards to the north, or even the rank swampy smell from the river which was thick as soup near the banks and so rich in chemicals that even the hardy carp had died.

Eddy Loyd liked to spend afternoons in the park in his old neighborhood. He never noticed the smells that changed on the shifting breeze. It was good to sit on the bench in the sun and let the neighborhood tongue waggers view his obvious success while the local street punks watched his blue Cadillac with hungry eyes and whispered to each other that you didn't mess with the snowman's wheels if you wanted to stay healthy.

Cocaine was the key to Eddy's success on Rice Street. It paid for the Cadillac, the three-hundred-dollar suits and the two bedroom pad he had several blocks east. More important to Eddy, it bought him what he always returned to the old neighborhood to find.

The girls in this neighborhood knew exactly what they had to sell by the time they were twelve and Eddy would buy if he had to, but buying never satisfied him like rape.

Catching one that was still a virgin was the best, but in this part of the city finding a street kid that was a virgin was as unlikely as a whore taking a busy Sunday off to go to church. The thing to do was offer them some free coke, a chance to get high, and when he got them to his apartment, the price of the coke was a surprise. Some of these kids even thought the coke would really be free when they knew everything had a price down here. But he always raped them, and then he got them high on coke and gave them a hit for later before he let them go. None of them ever turned him in, a couple had even gone back to his apartment a second time for the coke.

It was safe down here because no one talked to the cops, not even the kids. The one time he had raped a girl from uptown had been different. He had gotten her high afterward and even gave her a quarter gram for later, and she had still screamed rape at the first cop she saw. The bitch had cost him fifty big ones in attorney fees and he still did three

2

years upstate. Three years of being called baby raper and looks of contempt from the other cons, not to mention several beatings.

Now, he kept to the old neighborhood where he wouldn't be caught again. All he had to do was sit in the park and be patient.

The girl he was watching today was new in the neighborhood. He had seen her several times that summer, but always with some of that new bunch that had moved into one of the apartment buildings on the next block; bunch of Mexicans or Cubans, or something. Hell, you couldn't tell the difference anymore, not that it made any difference as long as they bought the dope he supplied to his ounce men and didn't butt into his territory. The girl was alone this time, wearing tight shorts and a halter that made her nipples stick out through the fabric. She was one of those who knew they looked good and liked to tease. She was asking for it around here, but she would act surprised when he showed her the knife and told her to get her clothes off.

The girl came toward him along the sidewalk, walking easy in sandals, with a fluid walk like a young cat. The only jewelry she wore was a single red stone on a leather lace around her neck, and she looked directly at him as she approached. Her high cheekbones and thin nose made him guess maybe she wasn't Cuban but he didn't think any more about it when she stopped in front of him and said softly:

"You have a cigarette, mister?"

"Sure, little lady," Eddy said. "I got something better than that to smoke here."

The girl smiled and joined him on the bench.

This one was going to be easy, Eddy thought. Smoke a little weed here, talk her into going to his apartment and he could do what he wanted with her. It would be good if she fought some. It was always better if they fought.

It had been a lousy summer for the boys at the River Station. In all their wisdom, the city fathers had decreed that the Third Ward would receive a new station house. It was not out of the generosity of their hearts or their love for the police, rather the results of some creative financing in which federal urban development funds could be used to upgrade a depressed area that included the police station.

The new station was erected next to the old, a four-story growth of steel, concrete, and glass that seemed out of place next to the weathered stone of the old station. It housed receiving, booking, administration, the patrolmens' muster room and several holding cells on the first floor. The detectives' briefing room, showers, locker room, and property room shared the second floor with records. The third floor was shared with the various detective squads and several interrogation rooms. The fourth floor was given over to special operation, internal security, the bomb squad, and a swat team that had never been put in operation through lack of funds.

The move to the new station had taken place in May, and demolition of the old station followed to make room for the police garage and parking lot. The River Station was now a modern wonder of offices with large windows, carpeted floors, central air conditioning, an elevator, and electronic security for the holding cells.

The cops hated it.

Never mind that the old station was a gloomy, shabby building with a leaky roof and grumpy plumbing that provided water, hot or cold, only when it felt like it. Never mind that the old station was a sweat box during the summer and an ice box during the winter. Never mind that they had grumped and bitched about the leaky roof, the plumbing, the heat or cold, every chance they had, not to mention the electrical system that usually failed when the fans were needed. That was normal. It was their right as public servants to bitch about their jobs, they were American workers who could bitch about the place they worked anytime they wanted. But, bad as it had been, the old station house had been a place with character, right down to the faded, moss green paint and the cockroaches. A frumpy old dowager that made them feel at home.

The new station was bright with glass, plastic, steel, and tile. It reminded them of a high-priced hooker, all glitter and efficiency but not a place where you could get comfortable. They took great delight in finding fault with the new building, pointing out that the air conditioning worked too well and was the cause of their summer colds, and that the new gas heating system was dangerous. They had smiled at each other with knowing grins when the high-tech, electronic lock-up had gone haywire and released everyone in the holding cells while locking the cops into the glass control center. They began to think that in time the new station house might develop a personality of its own; but they still didn't like the new station.

The job they had scheduled for that afternoon was not high on their popularity list either. There were lots of things they would rather do with their time other than kicking in the doors of people who sold drugs. People who sold drugs usually kept several guns around because they did not want to be robbed by unsavory characters who knew they wouldn't call the cops to report a robbery.

The problem was, a drug pusher found it difficult to tell the difference between some unsavory character kicking down the door to rob them and cops kicking down the door to arrest them. Not that it made any difference to the pushers, who operated on the theory that it was prudent to shoot first and let the coroner sort out the good guys from the bad guys.

Lieutenant Jaworski offered the opinion that it would be a fine idea to let Pat Runnion kick the door in since he had developed a real technique for the job. Runnion had mistakenly kicked in the wrong door at a local motel and surprised a district judge enjoying the services of a hooker whose case the judge was hearing the next day. To make matters worse, in the confusion that followed the real suspect escaped. "It was a mistake anyone could have made," Runnion told Jaworski.

"The judge didn't think so," Jaworski said.

The lieutenant was a man with a bald head and a pair of clear blue eyes that stabbed at you from under shaggy eyebrows. He was a broad shouldered, heavy man like cops had to be when he joined the force. He was putting on weight now from too many years behind a desk and his face was lined with suspicion and resentment from watching the crime rate go up and police support go down.

"I was thinking you and Lonto should go in together, it's your bust. The rest of the squad can back you up. Take some uniforms too if you need extra men."

The rest of the squad were scattered around the office. Pat Runnion and Tony Lonto were leaning against the file cabinets to the right of the office door, Pete Mills and Neil O'Malley sitting on the edge of the conference table, David Washington, the only new detective on the squad was sitting in a chair at the end of the lieutenant's desk while Vincent Gonzalez was perched on the low bookcase, watching Carl Pavolny, a narcotics detective from the Fourth Ward who was sitting in the chair directly in front of Jaworski's desk, a place of dubious honor. Detective Pavolny had been asked to attend the evening events as a matter of courtesy since the location of the pending bust was in a high crime area that was policed by both the Third and Fourth Ward stations. The six-man squad was supposed to enter the pusher's apartment with several patrolmen as back up.

"How about we let the narc here kick in the door?" Runnion asked, grinning at Pavolny. "He could demonstrate how the narcs of the flying Fourth do the job."

"Stick your door kicking where the sun don't shine," Pavolny said, flatly. "Better yet, let the spic there kick the door in, it's probably one of his cousin's places anyway."

"Be careful Detective Gringo," Vincent said, smiling coldly. "One of my cousins down there might cut your throat, mistaking you for a pig."

Vincent Gonzalez was a darkly handsome man, who everyone thought should be in the movies, or at least on TV. Runnion said that all the hookers on Pimps Row were eager to be arrested by Vincent and promised to do erotic things with his body if he would visit their apartments. Carl Pavolny, on the other hand was a surprisingly ugly man, with a bald head, a fat red face that was equipped with a broken nose and mean, dark eyes. He also had no neck. The squad members were reasonably sure that Pavolny had a neck, just like normal people, but they had never seen one. It appeared to them that his bald head was connected directly to Pavolny's fat body.

He stared at Vincent and grinned, showing large, yellow teeth. "Touchy little prick, ain't you?"

"Knock the crap off," Jaworski said. He stared at Lonto. "How about it, Lonto? You want to fill us in on who's the guest of honor for the party tonight?"

"The one and only Eddy Loyd," Lonto said. "Old Pimps Row boy who gave up pimping his sisters for a new trade."

"What the fuck is that?" Pavolny asked. "Jack-rolling?"

"We busted a guy pushing crack a few days ago and he said our boy Eddy is a big supplier of coke nowadays."

"You're going to kick a guy's door in on a tip from a fucking pusher trying to make a plea bargain?" Pavolny asked. "The punk would give up his mother to stay out of jail."

"Last year or so there's been a new coke source in the precinct," Lonto said, "and we've had some information that Eddy Loyd was the supplier. Trouble is, every time we've picked him up, he's been clean."

"Yeah, well maybe he's got a crystal ball, huh, Lonto?" Pavolny asked. "How about it Pancho, he got a crystal ball?" He grinned at Vincent.

"Maybe so," Vincent said mildly.

"So how's it going to be, Lonto?" Washington asked. "If no one else wants it, I'll kick the damn door in."

Washington was new on the squad but a veteran of six years on special operations at midtown. He was as tall as

Runnion but heavier, standing six feet three and weighing two hundred and forty pounds. He looked like he would enjoy kicking in doors.

"The man wants to be a hero," Detective Mills said.

"This isn't a debating team," Lonto said. "Runnion and I set this up, we'll take care of the door."

"What time do we go in?"

"At six," Lonto said. "Right in time for Eddy to be set up for the evening rush."

"Yeah, well he'll probably flush the junk before we can get in anyway." Pavolny said.

"Not this time," Lonto said. "Eddy's got the only apartment in the building. The others have been turned into offices or storage space. And at five-thirty the water's being turned off to the building. If we're lucky, Eddy won't have enough water to flush a roach."

"Is that legal?" O'Malley asked, grinning.

Lonto shrugged. "I didn't have it turned off. I just happen to know they're going to fix the pipes up the street and thought we should take advantage of it."

They grinned at each other. Even cops like something that seems slightly sneaky.

"Well, I got to take a leak before we get on with this," Pavolny said, heaving himself out of the chair. "Better call my girl while I'm at it. This crap will probably go on all night."

"What's the matter," Vincent asked. "Won't the señora allow you out late?"

"I got your señora swinging, Pancho," Pavolny said on his way out.

The rest of the squad decided on coffee before the fun began.

At five-forty-five the squad arrived at 903 4 Street. Lonto had decided that the six detectives from the squad, along with two patrolmen, and Detective Pavolny were enough men to make the bust. Since there were only two exits from the building, plus a rusting fire escape that one eager patrolman could cover with a shotgun, any more men on the team could get in each other's way and endanger them all. Lonto did not, in fact, expect that there would be shooting during the bust once Eddy Loyd was aware that they were police officers. From his record, it was obvious that Eddy liked to play it safe, and knew enough about the legal system to play his games with the courts and a high-priced lawyer, rather than risk a shoot-out. He had been arrested fifteen times, convicted once. With those odds, Eddy was not likely to start a fire fight, but no one was sure enough about that theory to take any chances.

The rough comradeship had drained out of the men when they were two blocks from the apartment, replaced by a grim silence as they moved swiftly through the building, guns drawn. Each team of two moved rapidly to their assigned positions. Lonto led the way up the stairs to the third floor apartment with Runnion close behind. Mills and O'Malley followed closely as back up with Pavolny trailing behind. Once on the third floor, speed was the goal.

Reaching Eddy Loyd's apartment, Lonto poised himself at the left of the door. Under the hall lights his face had the sharp look of a hunter, with his high cheekbones, thin nose, and cold eyes.

As Runnion braced himself against the wall opposite Eddy's door, he could taste the coppery fear that always gripped him before a bust. A fear he always knew would be there. He pushed off from the wall and put the weight of his body behind a kick next to the door lock.

The door sprang open, taking part of the jamb into the room.

"Police!" Lonto shouted. "No one moves!"

They were in an empty room.

The detectives quickly checked the other two rooms, shouting "Police" before they began to relax. The apartment was empty.

"Empty as a whore's charity box." Pavolny said. He was

sweating and breathing hard. "This must be a typical River Station tactic—empty apartments make safe busts!"

"Shove it, asshole," Lonto said.

"Better take a look at this, Tony," Mills said from the doorway of the bedroom. "We must have missed one hell of a party."

As Lonto walked to the door he was prepared to see almost anything from a naked lady to a dead zebra. A few years of finding week-old bodies in hot rooms, or freshly killed bodies stuffed into garbage cans, kept a man prepared to view ugly scenes.

The bedroom was not the complete mess he'd expected. It was not littered with bodies or stinking of old death; Lonto had certainly seen worse bedrooms. The bed was unmade, a man's shirt was on the floor next to the bed and the door to the closet was open as were the drawers in the dresser. It was a bedroom you could find in half the apartments in the city. What was unusual about this one was it appeared that someone had sprayed a good part of the room with blood. The sheets were soaked in a thick, jellylike puddle and the fanlike sprays of red reached up the wall at the head of the bed. A second, smaller pool of blood was shining wetly on the floor between the bed and the door.

"Better call the medical examiner and the lab boys," Lonto said.

"Well, well, what have we got here?" Pavolny said, pushing into the doorway. "This Eddy Loyd must play some kinky games."

"Someone does," Lonto said.

"Looks like someone tossed the place too," Pavolny offered. "Whoever it was didn't do much of a job."

"Maybe he's a lousy housekeeper," Lonto said.

"You sure that's blood?" Pavolny asked. "Could be paint."

"Does it smell like paint?" Lonto said, and noticed that Pavolny didn't smell so good either before he stepped away from the man.

"So maybe it's one of those new paints that don't stink."

"Maybe it's Easter egg dye, too," Mills said. "It's blood alright."

"So, what the hell have we got here?" Pavolny asked. "Did anyone look under the bed for a body?"

Lonto looked at Mills who carefully eased down on his knees and quickly looked under the bed.

"Nothing but dust."

"Well, it ain't a homicide," Pavolny said. "No dead meat, no homicide. It looks like you boys have a problem."

"Whatever lost that much blood has the problem," Mills added.

"Runnion," Lonto said, "stay here with Mills while the rest of us search the building. Someone get the patrolmen to check the alley and the garbage.

"What are we looking for?" O'Malley wanted to know.

"A body," Lonto said.

"One without blood," Pavolny added.

"Or a dead horse," Runnion said, getting into the act.

"Anything unusual," Lonto said, "and have someone check the roof."

They moved out of the apartment, leaving Runnion and Mills to study the abstract patterns of blood on the walls.

The initial search of the building produced nothing the police were interested in except the general opinion that the place was badly maintained and rapidly deteriorating as were the apartment buildings on each side.

Jim Brynt, the patrolman who had been assigned to guard the fire escape, and was then given the task of searching the alley for a discarded body was successful in locating a still warm body beside the garbage pile near the rear exit.

Brynt, eager to be a part of his first murder case had the shit scared out of him when the body sat up to protect a half empty bottle of wine from a nosy cop.

"Don't move," Brynt shouted, jumping back and leveling his riot gun.

"Get your own wine," the man said, trying to focus on Brynt. "You got a gun," he observed.

"What have you got?" Mills called from the entrance of the building.

"A drunk," Brynt answered.

Upstairs, Lonto saw the coroner, Charley Hooley, and the lab technicians push into the apartment.

"So, where's the body, Tony," he said. "I hope the goddamn thing ain't a week old."

"No body, Charley. At least we haven't found one yet."

"No body? Then what do you need me for?" Hooley asked. "I'm the meat man, remember? I get the old ones, or the ones in pieces. I got one now to put together that they brought me in two bags. I'm not even sure if he's all there or if some of him is still at the junk yard with his car."

"Sounds like a personal problem," Runnion said.

"So what am I doing here when you don't need me?"

"Take a look in there," Lonto said.

While Hooley was checking out the bloody bedroom, Brynt arrived upstairs with the drunk. Lonto and Runnion took him into the second bedroom where they could talk to him without wall-to-wall cops distracting him from the problem of remembering such details as his name. He was a gaunt man with dirty hair and a thin, partly gray beard. He was wearing a badly stained suit that had once been blue and a dirty shirt that was brown with dirt. His shoes were laced with string that matched the rope holding his pants up.

"What's your name?" Lonto asked.

"Yeah, who are you?" the man asked Runnion.

"He means you. What's your name?"

"Bill," the man said, feeling his pockets. "Name's Bill."

"What's your last name, Bill?"

Bill thought about it. "Russel," he finally said. "Yeah, Bill Russel, that's my name."

"What were you doing around here, Bill?" Lonto asked.

"It's my place," Bill said. "I got my mattress out there."

"Were you out there all day, Bill?"

"Except this morning," Bill said. "I had to go downtown this morning. You gonna keep my bottle? The cop in the alley took my bottle."

"Your bottle's okay," Lonto said. "You know Eddy Loyd?"

"Who's that?"

"The guy that lives here."

"He's the only guy that lives here," Bill said. "I don't know his name."

"Do you know him?"

"I know what he looks like," Bill said, firmly. "I don't know his name."

"Did you see him today?" Runnion asked.

He stared at them absently. "That's why I went downtown," he said. "I told you I went downtown didn't I?"

"Did he send you downtown for something?" Lonto asked.

"Nope," Bill said patiently. "He gave me the money and I went downtown to get a bottle. You sure that cop didn't take it?"

"What time did he give you the money?"

"This morning, when he went out."

"What time this morning?"

Bill looked at his wrist vacantly. "I ain't got a watch."

Lonto and Runnion exchanged glances.

"Did you see him after you got your bottle?" Runnion asked.

Bill shook his head. "I didn't see him after he came back."

"How do you know he came back if you didn't see him?" Lonto asked.

Bill looked at them reproachfully. "His car's here," he said. "I ain't a cop but I can see his car's here. Big fuckin' blue one."

"Did anyone else come into the building?"

"I was back there on my mattress," Bill said. "If I tell you something can I have my bottle back?"

13

"I'll personally make sure your bottle's safe," Lonto said. "What do you want to tell us?"

"He usually had a girl up there," Bill said. "He beat a couple of 'em up."

"Was there a girl with him today?"

Bill shrugged and scratched his crotch casually. He made Runnion want to scratch too.

Lonto shook his head. "What do you think?" he asked Runnion.

"Take him down to detox maybe," Runnion said. "He might remember more after he's sober."

Lonto nodded.

Hooley was finished in the bedroom as the detectives turned Bill over to the patrolmen for a trip down to the detoxification clinic. Lonto had no great hope that he would remember more when he sobered up, but a bath, food, and three days without booze couldn't hurt him.

As Hooley joined them, he said. "I'll get you a written report on the blood type but that's about all I can do. You want my opinion now?"

"Let's hear it," Lonto said.

"This one yours, Tony?"

"It started as our drug bust so it looks like we're stuck with whatever else it is now."

"If that's human blood, and it's my guess that it is, and if it all came from one person, then you probably have a homicide."

"If a body turns up," Runnion said.

"Looks like a large artery was cut, probably in the neck the way the blood was sprayed up the wall. Whoever it was probably died in a couple of minutes with their jugular cut. I'd say it started on the bed and the body ended up on the floor where the smaller pool of blood collected."

"Any chance of a person living after losing that much blood?" Lonto asked.

Hooley shook his head. "Awful lot of blood in there. My guess is that you got a dead one someplace."

"That's what I was afraid you'd say."

"Well, try to find it before it gets too ripe for a change, okay? I'll get a report over to you tomorrow."

"The lab finished here too?"

"Prints, photos, and samples all bagged and tagged. You guys can toss the place."

"Just what I wanted to do this evening," Runnion said.

"Have fun," Hooley said on his way out.

"Get them started in here, will you, Pat? I'm going down and search Loyd's car."

The car, as Bill had stated, was a new, blue Cadillac, parked illegally in the mouth of the alley near the front of the building and prudently locked. From a prowl car nearby, Lonto retrieved a long thin piece of flexible metal with a hook on one end, which they called a Mexican car key on the squad, and unlocked the Cadillac door on his first attempt, thinking he had a real talent at it, if he should ever want to take up car theft as a career.

He sat behind the wheel of the car a moment, remembering that the compact he drove was five years old, showing rust from the winter road salting, and badly in need of a tune-up and winterizing before the city froze solid. Judging from Loyd's car, the man was a successful dope pusher, but judging from the bedroom upstairs you could also argue that his success was, at the moment, questionable. But there was no doubt either that the man had never worked a day in his life and could afford a new car that the year's salary of a detective first grade couldn't buy.

Maybe he really should take up stealing cars, Lonto thought, as he began to search the car. After fifteen minutes, he had checked under the seats, floor mats, inside the ash trays and glove compartments, and had found nothing of interest but a gold coke spoon which had been behind the sunshield above the driver's seat. Now, lying on his back on the floor, he reached up to check behind the dash board.

The package was taped to the back of the tape deck.

"Yeah!" Lonto said to himself.

Pulling the package free, he unwrapped it on the seat and carefully counted eighteen smaller packages of cocaine. Cocaine, unless Loyd was packing powder sugar into one ounce bags these days.

"Well, the day wasn't a total loss," Runnion said, adding the cocaine to the evidence bag when Lonto returned to the apartment. "All we turned up here is a thirty-two caliber revolver and a phone book that might be his list of customers or contacts."

"Keep that and turn the rest in at the property room," Lonto said. "Guess we can wrap this up, huh?" He looked around. "Where the hell's Pavolny?"

"He took off an hour ago," Washington said. "Had to get back to his squad."

"I'll bet," Runnion said, picking up the evidence bag. "Well, let's get out of here. I got to get over to the hospital before visiting hours are over."

"How's she doing, Pat?" Lonto asked.

The 'she' he was referring to was Runnion's wife of three years who was now in St. Martin's waiting for a kidney that Pat couldn't give her. They had been waiting for a year now, the last four months with her in the hospital and Pat working seventy-hour weeks at two jobs, trying to keep up with the bills.

"She's hanging in there," Runnion answered. "Sometimes I think she's tougher than I am. The worst for her is not seeing Joey every day. That kid means the world to her. I miss him too."

"Lin's a fighter," Tony said. "She'll make it. Robin said you could bring Joey back from your folks and she would take care of him. You'd both get to see him more."

"Tell her thanks," Runnion said. "I'll talk to Lin about it."

"It's been a hell of a day," Lonto said as they got in the car.

2

Detective Carl Pavolny had not experienced an outstandingly good day either. Having been ordered over to the River Station to join in a drug bust had greatly upset his schedule, and very nearly screwed up his life when he learned Eddy Loyd was to be the main attraction of the evening's show.

Fortunately Eddy had not attended. Leaving Eddy's apartment building Pavolny had turned west until he reached U.S. 28 where it led into the strip area of the city on this side of the river. The Strip, or Pimps Row as the cops fondly called it, began at U.S. 28 and followed both banks of the river, its heart stretching from the highway to Sixty-first Street where Davis Drive cut it off from downtown and the three-hundred block ran into Davis on the south side where the city got better.

From where the bookie leaned against the stairs railing that led down into the Crazy Eight pool hall, he could view all the evening traffic along that block of the strip. He recognized Pavolny as soon as he got out of his car farther up the block. He had no desire to talk to any cop this evening, not with his pockets full of the day's action. But down here there were two types of cops, the tough, straight ones, who wouldn't take a free cup of coffee on a cold night, and the tough, mean ones who would take everything you had until they bled you dry before they busted your ass. Pavolny had a reputation for being one of the tough, mean ones, who, at the moment was in the process of putting the heat on one of the local pushers.

Clearly, Pavolny was in fact giving the pusher heat as he shoved him back against the wall and and shouted at him. The pusher was a successful ounce man named Joe Wells. On the street he was known as Joe the Dog, a local boy who supplied the dime and quarter bag men with their daily supply of cocaine to turn into the fast-selling crack that was the drug of choice on the Strip lately.

As Pavolny shoved the pusher into his car, the bookie hoped he hadn't been caught with his week's supply of cocaine on him or he'd sure as hell be short when he paid his supplier off that week. And coming up short with the cocaine money would get you very dead on the strip. The bookie shrugged and went down into the pool hall to get the day's game scores.

Down the block, after he turned into a side street, Pavolny tossed the pusher's cocaine back into his lap as he drove. He figured he had to make it look good when he busted one of his men on the street. He parked under an overpass as Joe the Dog lit a cigarette.

Joe was known all along the strip as a steady bag man, and most of the addicts in the area tried to stay on his good side because he was also known to carry a butterfly knife and possessed an ugly temper. He carried the knife in a drop sheath on his wrist, where a twist of the wrist would drop the knife into his waiting hand so that he was always ready to give a slow-paying addict a slashed face or throat. Nobody wanted to ever short pay Joe the Dog which was why he was one of Pavolny's best dealers. On the other hand, if you worked for a son of a bitch like Pavolny, the way you stayed healthy was to do what you were told and keep the money right.

"What the hell you doing down here, boss?" Joe the Dog asked.

"Looking for that asshole Eddy," Pavolny said. "The cops

from the River Station just hit his apartment and by now they have a warrant out on him."

"Jesus! Didn't you warn him?"

"I called from the station and he wasn't there," Pavolny said. "Worse yet his pad looked like a butcher shop, blood all over. Now he's on the hot list and I just gave him a half kilo last night."

"How bad is this?" Joe asked, looking up from counting the bags of cocaine as he put them back into his pocket. "Should we stop dealing for awhile?"

Joe was perhaps thirty years old, or maybe a street-worn twenty-five. In any event he was tough, mean, and streetwise enough to know that pushing dope for a cop on the inside was one of the safer ways to deal. Inside information could keep you ahead of any drug busts, leaving only the other rip-off artists on the street to worry about. Even those could be dealt with, just as the competition was, a word to Pavolny and the competition found themselves getting busted by cops who seemed to know exactly when and where they were selling dope. After all, all's fair in love and the cocaine trade. Joe had met Pavolny through his wife Windy Sterling who's real name was Erma Perkins from South Atkins. Windy was a hard-working hooker who'd grown quickly tired of supporting both of them on her back and had suggested to Pavolny that he could use an extra man on the street one afternoon when he stopped by for a freebie. Working with Pavolny lasted longer than his marriage had, which did not bother Joe at all since he had realized at the tender age of twelve that money and drugs would buy any woman on the Strip.

Pavolny was one of the few people who knew how to keep Joe loyal and honest. It was a combination of protection and greed and the fact that if all else failed he would feed him into the dog food grinder over at the stockyard.

"I'll tell you when we slow down and when the heat's

on," Pavolny said. "Did you hear anything about Eddy on the street?"

"No," Joe said, shaking his head. "I know he's always bringing some young gash up to his pad. Maybe he figured she would yell rape this time and took her out."

"That's all we need," Pavolny said. "If he gets busted on a murder charge you know who he's going to finger for the cops to make a deal?"

"Yeah. Us," Joe whispered.

"And he knows all three of us. Me, you, and JR."

"You talk to JR yet?"

"I'll see him later," Pavolny said. "That fuckin' JR even knows I bring the stuff in from Florida."

"We're in deep shit if they pick him up. Can't you do anything about it from your end?"

"Not a chance. The case belongs to River Station and I wouldn't take a chance at burying the case with that wop fuck Lonto on it."

"So what do we do?" Joe wanted to know.

Pavolny let his eyes search the shadows outside the car. Behind them the lights of Pimps Row were reflecting against the sky.

"I think our friend Eddy has become a very large problem to our little organization, and you know how we deal with problems."

"Yeah. Dog food," Joe said, and smiled. He had never liked that slimy baby raper anyway.

"It would be nice if our problem did leave our city," Pavolny said. "Put himself beyond the reach of the police so to speak."

"Maybe that's not such a good idea, the dog food I mean," Joe said. "If Eddy don't turn up the case stays open, don't it? And from what you say about this Lonto prick, he'll keep digging."

"You might be right," Pavolny said. "Be better if he turns up in some alley where they can identify him. A body will close the case alright."

"They'll figure it was a drug rip-off."

"First things first," Pavolny said. "First we got to find him. You got any ideas where he'd hole up?"

"If he's running from the cops, he probably figures you'll be looking for him, too, especially if he lost your coke. He'll be hard to find."

"He ain't smart enough to leave town," Pavolny said. "So put some people on it, get him located."

"Just located?"

"Get him out of our hair, man," Pavolny said. "You do that and you can take over his territory, too, along with a nice bonus."

Joe grinned. "I'll find him. I've been wanting a chance like this since he conned my cousin's girl up to his pad, not that she was a cherry or anything."

"Well, get on it tonight then," Pavolny said. "The quicker Eddy's down at the morgue the safer we'll be."

"You going to put JR out lookin' too?" Joe asked.

"It's his neck just like it's ours," Pavolny grinned. "Can't you stand some competition?"

"Shit, I'll find Eddy," Joe assured him. "JR deals with the suburb bunch. Eddy won't hole up over there. And for a few hits of crack I'll have lots of creeps out looking for him tonight."

In the morning, Lonto enjoyed the walk from the crosstown bus stop on Davis Drive. It was the time of the year he would like to take a weekend off to spend in the country with Robin. As he approached, he viewed the new station house with dislike.

Well, maybe we'll get used to it, he thought. Maybe fifty years from now some rookie will think this station house has character, like I thought the old one did when I first started working here. Not likely though, a four-story box of glass and concrete will take more than fifty years to develop any character like the old place always had.

Lonto had taken the bus in to work that morning only

because Robin had decided it was time to tune-up and winterize the car as he had promised to do each week for the past month. Her decision was made based on the fact that the frost last night had killed the last remaining flower in the box outside the apartment window. She had stated firmly that freezing weather was only a few weeks away, despite what the weather man promised, and Lonto could not argue with Robin's logic.

He pushed through the front doors of the station house and into receiving. The building still had a new smell, hospital-like and cold this morning. The high receiving and booking counter, with a heavy screen partition was on his left, the entrance into the holding cells was on the right behind the heavy steel door. Sergeant Tom Wolverton sat behind his own desk in the booking area bent over the daily assignment book with a steaming cup of black coffee near his right hand. Wolverton was a man in his late fifties, thin and balding, wearing the steel-framed glasses that made him appear more of an aging school teacher rather than a cop close to retirement who had three medals of valor in his personal file and two bullet scars on his body. He looked up as Lonto walked passed the counter.

"You got banker's hours this week?"

"How goes it, Tom," Lonto said. "Anything interesting come down last night?"

"Not according to the booking sheet," Wolverton said. "But who knows what the desk sergeant at night didn't write down."

"Well, they can't all be good as you, Tom. You wouldn't have anything to bitch about if they did."

"Tell O'Malley that if he's going to book that guy he brought in this morning he should get him down here."

"Already. He must have busted him between his place and here."

"At breakfast he said."

"I hope it's not going to be one of those days," Lonto said, and shook his head. He ignored the elevator and began his climb up to the third floor, taking his time and wondering when the new paint smell would fade in the stairwell. The decorators had decided on two colors for the building: blue and yellow. The halls and stairwells were painted blue on the bottom and an odd yellow above. The colors met on the walls about shoulder high and no one on the squad was as happy about the colors as the decorators had been. It was Detective Mills's opinion that the painters had unloaded on the city the two colors no one else would buy. Reaching the third floor Lonto turned left down the hall where the detective squadroom overlooked the garage.

The blue-and-yellow combination had been continued in the squad room but there was no doubt it was a squad room. There were cluttered desks, ringing phones, and battered file cabinets against one wall, which were packed with badly typed and sometimes misfiled case files and rap sheets of past and present criminals working the precinct. The desk areas were originally divided by movable partitions that were supposed to offer privacy to work and dampen the noise. After one day of having to get up from their desks and walk around partitions to talk to another squad member they had moved the partitions into the briefing room down the hall and enjoyed their large open room where they, too, could see what was going on around them. The noise in the squad room was as much a part of being a cop to Lonto as wearing a gun.

Detective Pat Runnion was perched on the corner of his desk watching O'Malley and Mills questioning a man in front of a heavy screen detention area that was an eight-by-eight-foot screen box with metal benches bolted to the floor. The cage was empty at the moment but Lonto knew that before the day was over it would be occupied briefly by various criminals and suspects before they were taken downstairs for booking and the holding cells.

Next to Runnion, Lonto seemed small. He was not a small man, he only appeared smaller compared to the other detectives on the squad who tended to be big beefy men with thick bodies rather than the more athletic build of Lonto, who was just under six feet with wide shoulders and narrow hips. Runnion insisted that while he wasn't built for breaking down doors, it was great to have a partner who could outrun quick-footed creeps. Lonto's dark complexion and thin features made him appear Arabic, giving the squad an opportunity to suggest that in reality he was a rich Arab with oil fields and harems who just worked as a cop for entertainment.

Lonto slipped his jacket off, hanging it on the back of his chair, nodded to Runnion, and asked. "So what's going on with that one?"

"You mean Cockroach Charley over there?"

"Cockroach Charley?"

"Real name is Charley Powell," Runnion said, grinning. "Used to work the restaurants uptown with the fly-in-my-food con game, only he would use a cockroach."

O'Malley waved at him, left Mills questioning the man and walked over to them saying, "You might want to talk to this guy, Tony."

"What's going on?" Lonto asked.

"You won't believe this," O'Malley said. "I stop at my usual eating spot this morning like usual. I've been going there for years. They see me come in the door and they know I'm gonna have eggs, bacon, and toast like usual. So I stop there and I'm waiting for my breakfast when I notice this guy here in a booth. He's about finished with his breakfast and he takes this little bottle out of his pocket and dumps something on what's left of his pancakes. So I'm wondering what this guy's up to when he stands up and demands to see the manager. Acts real upset and starts shouting at Mary, she's the waitress there, that there's a bug in his food and threatening to sue them."

"What happened?" Runnion asked.

"Jerry, the manager, comes out and tries to calm the man down. Even apologizes, saying he'll give him a free breakfast of his choice. This jerk over there is a great actor, all red-faced and indignant, says he wouldn't eat anything there. Then, he says he might be interested in a free meal at some other restaurant and perhaps a ten spot would be satisfactory."

"Nice touch," Lonto said, "that way he gets a free meal there and puts booze money in his pocket. What did you do?"

"I figured I didn't need some jerk putting the squeeze on my breakfast joint. I walk over and flash my badge and tell Jerry I saw the creep put the cockroach on his plate," O'Malley said. "And when I shake him down, he's got this bottle in his pocket with three or four more cockroaches in it. The guy must figure he'll never have to pay for a meal as long as the cockroaches last."

O'Malley was enjoying himself. He was thinking that all his days should start like this, a bust before breakfast. Then he realized he hadn't eaten any breakfast, and decided he had been screwed out of his one peaceful meal of the day.

"Anyway," he went on. "You won't believe what I found in this creep's other pocket."

"More cockroaches?" Runnion asked.

"Four more bottles alright," O'Malley said. "But they got crack in them! We can get this silly bastard as a pusher."

Lonto grinned. "Crack, huh? Sweat him some and see if he'll give up his supplier." He turned to Runnion. "Have you got that address book you picked up at Loyd's apartment last night?"

"Right here," Runnion patted his pocket.

"I figure we should start with those," Lonto said. "One of them might know where we can find him."

"Shit!" Runnion said. "I almost forgot. The lieutenant wanted to see you soon as you got here."

"What now?" Lonto said, and headed for Lieutenant Jaworski's office adjoining the squad room.

Normally, Lieutenant Jaworski would only be in charge of a detective squad. At the smaller River Station, he was responsible for the operation of the entire station, a position that would require a captain's rating at Midtown. Jaworski had, in fact, been offered his captain's bars on two occasions and had flatly turned the promotion down when he learned that the captain's rating required a transfer to head one of the other precincts in the city.

The lieutenant knew that River Station was the hot spot of the city despite its size and he wouldn't trade it for any desk job in any suburban precinct or at Midtown. He knew that the cops who came to River Station and stayed more than six months were good cops and in this part of the city they had to be good just to survive. He was wondering now if one of his cops had gone bad when Lonto entered the office.

"Sit down, Tony," he said. "What in hell went down on this drug bust last night?"

"It's all in the report, Lieutenant," Lonto said. "Nobody in the apartment, but the place looked like a butcher shop."

"Any report from the lab yet?"

Lonto shook his head, wondering what was going on. Jaworski usually called the team in to brainstorm a case. If you were called to Jaworski's office alone, it usually meant you were on the carpet. Or as the lieutenant always said, "Crap runs downhill, and when I get it, my cops are going to get it." Lonto wondered where he had screwed up.

"Hooley didn't have any doubt it was human blood," he said. "And he figured who ever lost it was dead."

Jaworski opened a box on his desk and took out a short, black cigar that Lonto knew was a sure sign that the lieutenant was upset. One of the squad had once stated the cigars looked like dog turds and smelled worse, but Lonto was never bothered by the smell. He was always bothered by an ass chewing, which Jaworski was a master at giving.

Jaworski watched Lonto as he lit his cigar. "Did the whole team search the apartment?"

"Everyone but Pavolny and the patrolmen," Lonto said. "I searched the car outside alone."

"Yeah," Jaworski said. "Report said that's where the cocaine was found. Taped in back of the radio."

"In back of the tape deck." Lonto said.

"Whatever," the lieutenant said, and took an evidence bag out of his desk drawer. "What did you do with the cocaine after that?"

"Made out an evidence tag and took it back upstairs. Why?"

"You keep it in your possession when you went back to the apartment?"

Lonto thought about it. "Sure," he said. "In the apartment I put it in the evidence bag."

"Did you keep the evidence bag then?"

"Well, no. It was on a coffee table in the living room while we finished and then we brought it in to the station."

"Cut the crap, Tony. Runnion was the one who turned it in, did anyone else have the evidence bag at anytime?"

"What's this about, Lieutenant?" Lonto asked. "Any one of us had access to it. You know how it is on a bust."

"That's what I was afraid of," Jaworski sighed.

As Lonto watched, Jaworski dumped the evidence bag onto his desk top.

"Count them." Jaworski ordered.

Lonto carefully counted the one-ounce packages. Then, looking puzzled, he counted them again. "Sixteen," he said.

Handing Lonto an evidence tag Jaworski said, "You logged eighteen one-ounce packages."

"Maybe I miscounted," Lonto said, not wanting to consider the other option.

"Bullshit," Jaworski said. "Don't hand me that crap. There's two ounces of cocaine missing from the time you picked it up, to here."

"I could have miscounted," Lonto said stubbornly. "It's happened."

"Damn it, Lonto!" Jaworski said. "This isn't the first time drugs have been missing around here. This is three times, count 'em, three times, these evidence bags have come up short in the last two months! The evidence room has been tapped too."

"What?"

"That's right. Usually on a bust where everyone on the squad is present but someone is getting into the evidence room regular. There could be more that I don't know about. And I'm not going to buy miscounts of evidence." Jaworski pounded on his desk. "One of ours is crooked, Lonto."

"They're all good men."

"I know that," Jaworski said. "But one of them is putting dope in his own pocket."

"Lieutenant, I know these guys. Hell, I trust them with my life."

"And you can still trust them," Jaworski said. "But one of them is a thief, and our job is to catch thieves even if they're our own."

"Have you called in Internal Security on this?" Lonto asked.

"Not yet," Jaworski said. "I'd rather we cleaned our own house. I don't want my cops thinking I'll bring the headhunters in here after them."

"So what are you going to do?" Lonto asked.

"You mean what are we going to do, Tony. Right now I figure you're my best bet on this."

"I'm not going to spy on the squad."

"I didn't think you would, but between the two of us I think we can set up a trap for whoever it is."

"What did you have in mind?"

"Do I have to do all the thinking around here?" Jaworski asked. "We create a situation where dope can be ripped off and we make sure everyone on the squad knows about it. Then we let our man bust himself."

"I don't like this," Lonto said.

"It's either that or the headhunters." Jaworski said. "Take your choice."

"I'm in," Lonto said. "But I still don't like it."

* * *

When Lonto returned to the squad room forty minutes later, Runnion had checked the names in Loyd's address book against the known criminals file at the station. Not surprisingly, eight of the twenty-two names belonged to felons, five were names of women living in the area, and nine were men with no records. It was Runnion's opinion that they should begin questioning the men with records in their attempt to locate the elusive Eddy Loyd.

"Twenty-two of them, huh?" Lonto said. "Maybe we should ask Jaworski to put another team on this. It'll take forever to question them all."

"Fat chance of help," Runnion said. "The other teams are tied up too." He studied Lonto a moment, then asked, "What did Jaworski want?"

"Wanted to know what went on at Loyd's apartment, since we're listing it as a probable homicide." Lonto studied the list of names. "Let's start with Frank Novak here, he's been busted a couple of times for pushing. Lives over on Sixty-fifth Avenue North according to this."

"That's over in the projects isn't it?"

"Yeah, he must be living with a welfare widow," Lonto said. "Let's go."

The smells inside one of the city's low-rent housing buildings are the same as those permeating the walls and stairwells of every run-down apartment building in the city. The odor of cooking, dirty clothes, urine, and decaying garbage. The odor seems to hang in the air and soak into the clothing and hair, the smell of living poor on a state welfare check and getting by without such luxury items as washing machines and disinfectant. The smell would hang around you long after you had left the building. The smell was waiting for them as they entered the building.

Checking the mailboxes, Runnion said, "This must be it, Novak Two-C. At least it's not on the top floor."

Lonto pushed open the inner door and walked toward the

steps. The area under the steps was being used as a convenient garbage dump, collecting paper bags and plastic sacks that leaked the rich odor of ripe garbage and the slow buzzing of the last of the year's flies. Down the hall leading to the rear exit a child's tricycle lay on its side and behind one of the doors a baby was crying loudly. On the second floor two teenagers in jeans and T-shirts were sharing a can of beer on the fire escape at the end of the hall and vanished quickly at the sight of Lonto and Runnion. On the identical doors the apartment numbers had been stenciled, and to the right of each door was a metal frame that held the resident's name.

Lonto and Runnion stopped at the first door on the right side of the hall, checking the name.

"Here's Novak."

"How do you want to do this?" Lonto asked.

"He's a felon, isn't he?"

"Hasn't been arrested for a couple of years though," Lonto said.

"That doesn't mean he's clean," Runnion said, pulling his service revolver out.

They positioned themselves on each side of the door, standing silent for a moment while they tried to hear any sounds from the apartment.

"Sounds like a TV's on in there," Lonto said, and used his left hand to knock on the door.

"Who is it?" a voice asked after a moment.

"Police. Open up please," Lonto said.

"Sounds like a woman," Runnion said.

"What do you want?" the voice asked.

"We'd like to talk to Frank Novak." Lonto said.

"He's asleep," the voice said. "Just a minute."

After several minutes they heard footsteps approaching the door, and then the chain lock on the door rattled. The door opened a crack and an eye peered out at them.

"Can't a guy get any sleep. What the hell's the matter?"

"You Frank Novak, aren't you?"

"Yeah. So?"

"We'd like to ask you some questions."

"What about?" Novak asked. "Don't I know you?"

"We've met," Lonto said, showing his badge.

"Yeah, okay," Novak said. "You guys never leave a man alone do you?"

"You want to do this the hard way, Novak?" Lonto asked.

"I'm clean," Novak said. "I don't have to talk to you."

"If we have to come back with a warrant we won't be so friendly," Lonto said. "How about letting us in, Frank?"

"Yeah, okay," Novak said. "I don't have to let you in here you know, not without a warrant."

"Yeah, we know," Runnion said.

"So how about it?" Lonto asked.

"Ah, shit! Jesus, you pricks never let up do you? A guy gets a record and you cops figure you can push him around anytime." He moved away from the door and took off the night chain.

There were dirty clothes draped over the couch and several toys scattered around the room. The woman stood in the bedroom door holding a baby that was wearing only a shirt and chewing on a chocolate cookie. She wore a loose house-dress.

"You in trouble again, Frank?" the woman asked.

"Get in the bedroom," Novak said. "Stay the hell out of this."

Novak was a tall, thin man with a pock-marked face and thin black hair. His nose was broken and there was a thick ridge of scar tissue on the bone under his eyebrows.

"What's this all about?"

"This is about your old pal, Eddy Loyd," Lonto said.

"I never heard of him."

"Sure you did," Runnion said. "He's the slime ball that's been supplying you with coke."

"Coke! What do you mean? I ain't pushing nothing anymore. I got me a regular job now." Novak looked first at Lonto, then Runnion. "I'm clean, man!"

"Where do you work at?" Runnion asked.

"The Star Arcade on River Street," Novak said.

"Star Arcade, huh," Lonto said. "Sure, we know the place, right, Runnion?"

"That's the place on our hot list isn't it?" Runnion asked. "Place where they been selling crack to the kids who hang out there. Fact is I think one of the kids died from an overdose a few weeks ago."

"That sounds like a place you'd work," Lonto said, watching Novak.

"Look, guys," Novak said. "I'm an ex-con. I got to work where I can get a job. I swear I ain't pushing."

"How about Eddy Loyd?"

"Okay, okay, so I know him," Novak said. "I know lots of guys. What about him."

"When did you see him last?" Lonto asked.

"I don't know. A few days ago I guess. He usually hangs around on River Street. I have a beer with him once in awhile."

"Just a casual friend, huh?"

"I wouldn't say we're friends," Novak said.

"Then why do you think he had your name and address in his little black book?" Runnion asked. "You two been doing some business?"

"I don't do any business with Loyd," Novak said. "You know how it is, what he does, he does with his own people."

"You're not one of them, huh?"

"We talked once," Novak said. "Maybe that's when he wrote my name down."

"What did you talk about?"

"Said he might be able to get me a job."

"What kind of job?" Lonto asked.

Novak shrugged. "Who knows," he said. "Was just bullshit anyway. He never called me."

"Who does Loyd usually hang around with?" Runnion asked.

"Hell, I don't know. I've seen him around with lots of guys."

"Want to think about that again?" Lonto asked. "Because if you don't come up with some names you're going down to the station."

"Look, I didn't do anything," Novak said. "You guys can't arrest me because I know Loyd."

"Try us," Runnion said.

"We want some names," Lonto said.

"I told you I don't know any names," Novak said. "Shit, okay. I seen him around with Joe the Dog quite a bit. That's all I know."

"What's his real name?" Runnion asked.

"Joe the Dog, that's his name. That's what people call him."

"We'll check it out." Lonto said, nodding at Runnion.

"And if we find out you're involved with Loyd in any way we'll be back," Runnion said.

"You guys always come back," Novak said behind them.

Detective Hooley was having a moderately successful day. Moderately successful, for an assistant medical examiner in Hooley's opinion, was not having a floater that had been in the river several weeks, or a body in several pieces to assemble. He had managed to piece together the car crash victim from yesterday and could turn his attention to less gory things such as the bloody bed sheets from Eddy Loyd's apartment.

In the laboratory, a bloody bed sheet could tell you several things besides the fact that the sheets badly needed washing. Examination of this particular bed sheet produced the information that the blood type was O, which was not a lot of help since 45 percent of all white people have O type blood. Further examination added the sheet was stained with semen, not unexpected on a bed sheet, and two distinct types of head hair, as well as a single pubic hair, all of which would

33

add more information to the file after examination in the laboratory.

Unfortunately, the sheet could not provide Hooley with enough cold hard facts, to prove in court that a homicide had taken place. At least, Hooley would not sign a report to that effect, simply because in this state, the laws require that there be a dead body to bring a charge of murder against any person.

Hooley could, and did sign a report to the effect that there was enough physical evidence to indicate a strong possibility that a homicide, and/or an extremely severe injury to persons unknown took place in the bedroom of the suspect's apartment, which was enough information for the police to issue a warrant for Eddy Loyd's arrest, so they could ask him such pointed questions as, "Where's the body?"

Along with the report, Hooley had several very good fingerprints gathered from around the apartment. Most, he was sure, would belong to the suspect, but one set of prints from the bedroom were surely those of a woman or a child and possibly those of the victim in this case, providing the prints would provide them with an identification.

One copy of all the prints was sent to the State Criminal Identifications Bureau, another to the FBI who boasted the largest collection of fingerprints in the country. And finally a copy went in the file for Lonto at the River Station. Hooley sent the tentative findings off to the proper departments before he turned to the more detailed examination of the body hair found on the sheet. On Lonto's copy of his report he added a note stating that in all likelihood they did indeed have a homicide on their hands.

Lonto, for one, had not doubted for a moment that someone had been murdered in Eddy Loyd's apartment. There had been the raw feel of violent death to the room, a feeling that he sensed and that his years as a cop warned him not to ignore.

There was also the feeling that Eddy Loyd had made him,

personally, look like a fool. Not that the other cops on the squad hadn't kicked in the doors of apartments before and rushed in only to find empty rooms, used syringes, and roaches waiting for them. But in this case, he had set up the stake-out to determine the most opportune time of the bust, a time when Loyd's business was at its best. He, personally, had determined that the time to hit the apartment was when the water to the building was turned off. It should have been a textbook bust rather than a bust that made him look like a horse's ass.

True, the bust had not been a total loss, they did have enough cocaine to charge Loyd with a dealer's rap. And enough further evidence to also bring a possible charge of homicide against him. Unfortunately, they did not have Eddy Loyd.

To make the bust worse, two ounces of cocaine from the evidence bag were missing and Lonto knew they were about to set up a situation that would trap one of their own. A sting operation was a standard procedure to use against a criminal. Planting one against a fellow cop made the operation distasteful.

He thought it was especially distasteful because he had remembered that Runnion had been in charge of the evidence bag in the apartment, and had later taken the bag from the apartment and checked it into property room.

But Pat was a good honest cop, he thought.

"I think this is one of the nights when you brought the job home with you," Robin said.

They had just finished eating dinner.

He smiled at her, still surprised even after almost a year of marriage, that this beautiful dark-haired woman was his wife. His once firm decision that a cop, especially him, should not be married had worn rapidly away after he met Robin. Her logic was that being married to a cop could be no worse than being married to a soldier, or a fireman, or even a construction worker, or for that matter a cab driver in this city. A wife worried about her husband coming home safe no matter what he chose for a career.

"Sorry," he said. "I guess my mind has been on this new case." He had learned, after just a few months together, that she was able to read his moods and seemed to instinctively know when to wait and when to talk. Their talks usually consisted of her listening intently while he told her about whatever problem was troubling him. It was a new experience for him, to share his thoughts with someone, to express his doubts and fears to another person, and to feel safe doing that.

She sat down next to him and kissed him, then snuggled against his chest.

"Want to talk?" she asked.

He sighed.

"I'm worried about Pat," he said finally.

"Is Lin worse?" Robin asked.

"No, nothing like that," Lonto said. "Last time you were out to see her, did she mention money problems?"

"Sure they have money problems, we all do," Robin said. "But with Pat working two jobs they'll make it. She worries about him being so tired all of the time."

"They have insurance for most of the hospital bills, don't they?"

Robin thought about it.

"I'm not sure if the insurance will cover the transplant. Why?"

"Just something that came up at the station," he said.

Later, after they had made love, Lonto lay awake staring at the dark, wondering if his partner had given in to the pressure of too many bills to pay and too little money to reach from payday to payday. Even a good cop could be tempted by the easy money of dope or bribes when someone they loved needed more than they could provide.

Lonto wished he could be sure who would end up busted in Jaworski's trap.

3

It was ten o'clock that evening before Joe the Dog left his apartment. Joe was a night person through habit and choice. He hated the streets during the daylight hours when the working stiffs crowded the sidewalks and the cops could see your action two blocks away. Daytime wasn't fit for anything but those silly fucks who worked for a living, except when a man could be inside a bar or pool hall.

Nighttime now, nighttime was the time for the action, the time for the players to be out and for the working slobs to creep from their dim little houses to the bright lights and shadows hoping to find some excitement and escape the dullness of their lives. Nighttime was the time for Joe to be on the streets selling them their dreams.

But not tonight.

Tonight, Joe had more personal business and pleasure. He left his apartment and drove down to the River Street section of the city, enjoying himself as he viewed the territory that would soon be putting money in his pocket rather than paying off to that slime ball Eddy.

It was better down here than it was in his section of the city. The apartment buildings were more run-down and the dives along the street sold watered whiskey that the B-girls kept the customers buying. Plus the fact that there were more ten-dollar hookers on the street than any place in the city. It all added up to the fact that the poorer the neighborhood was, the more crack they would buy to escape. The money down here was right for a player who knew how to work the streets. It was twenty after eleven, when Joe the Dog parked his car off the corner of Rice Street.

The night sky was darker than usual, with blue flashes of lightning lighting the sky to the north. Off Rice Street were block after block of the boxlike apartment buildings separated by narrow, trash-filled alleys. Most of the buildings were occupied, in some a family shared a one-room apartment with a hot plate for a kitchen and a bathroom down the hall that was used by twenty other families on that floor. Other one-room apartments served as a place to sleep for a dozen adults who lived on the streets during the day. A housing inspector once said the area was as densely populated as Hong Kong or a Cambodian refugee camp. The people in the area sat on fire escapes, or on the front steps of the building while the kids played in the streets and alleys.

The action on Rice Street was in the packed bars and pool halls, while the hustlers worked the crowds on the sidewalks and the players sold blow at fifty bucks a gram or crack at ten bucks a vial. The streets were crowded with people and the alleys crawled with rats and roaches.

Joe the Dog smiled to himself as he walked toward the café where José Lopez would meet him. He could see the hustlers along the street who specialized in mugging and jack-rolling eyeing him. Some of them, fifteen- or sixteen-year-old kids with old eyes, were wondering how easy it would be to jump the white-faced prick who looked like he had business in the neighborhood. It seemed easy to pull him into a doorway or alley where a flash of a knife or the thump of a pipe would put the evening's money in their pocket. Easy, except there was a cocky sureness about this one, a sense of menace in the smile and cold eyes that watched everything around him. It wasn't smart to jump a street-wise red-neck asshole who should be kept chained in the barn on the farm, not one who came down here hoping for the chance to cut off some hard working spic's balls. Worse yet, some of those red-necks carried a big fuckin' gun and would blow your ass away in a hot second.

Joe the Dog walked through the crowds with no problem. Only the hookers smiled at him. One, a young coffee-colored girl with an overripe figure asked, "How about it mister? Twenty bucks will get you something you never had before."

"What have you got? AIDS?" Joe asked, pushing her aside and grinning at her pimp as he walked past. The pimp decided there was no problem and glared at his whore.

José Lopez had called him at his apartment this afternoon asking if the word on the street was true, because if Joe was giving away an ounce of blow to find Eddy Loyd, then he knew where the prick was holed up. Lopez was one of the street pushers who worked the Spanish trade down there. An independent pusher who Joe had supplied a few times and who was now willing to help him put Eddy out of business, thereby making more business for himself. A classic method of dealing with competition. But when Joe took over this territory, he knew he would either put Lopez on his payroll or the little spic would be dog food. That also was one of the classic risks you took in doing business.

The address José Lopez had given Joe, was three buildings down off the corner of Seventh and Rice, a small, combination coffee shop and grocery store where Latin music pounded over the men playing cards at the tables. There were eighteen men playing cards when Joe walked through the front door. Leave it to fuckin' Lopez to want to meet with a bunch of long-haired greasers, Joe thought. All these spics stick together. But Lopez was a player and wouldn't try to pull any shit.

The men playing cards stared at him a moment when he walked in, their faces expressionless. They returned to their game after a moment as though it was usual to see a white face in there. A pretty, dark-eyed girl sat behind a counter on his left where groceries were sold. She studied him openly, with a hint of a smile.

"José Lopez around here?" Joe asked, wondering if any of these pricks spoke English.

"You are Joseph Wells?" the girl asked.

"Yeah, I'm Wells."

She smiled at him. "He is in back," she said. "Go through the back door there," she pointed.

"Okay, thanks," Joe said.

The girl turned away to speak to a customer as he walked toward the back of the café.

Joe the Dog pushed open the door and stepped outside, stopping in surprise as the door behind was pushed shut and locked. He stared at the small fire burning in what had once been a private courtyard. Being a city boy, Joe had never seen an open fire in his life, fire was something that ate buildings and sometimes people. He stared in fascination.

The fire had been built near the center of a small cobblestone courtyard that had been swept clean of debris and garbage. The flickering light reflected off the surrounding buildings, making moving shadows around the circle of light at the fire. One man sat cross-legged at the fire facing him and two others stood just at the edge of the fire light.

"Lopez! You prick. What's going on here?" Joe asked.

There was no answer as Joe listened to his voice echo hollowly in the courtyard.

"What kind of fuckin' game is this," Joe wanted to know. He could feel sweat on his face, knowing something was very wrong with this set-up.

Not being a fool, he turned quickly and tried the door frantically, even though he knew it would be locked. He turned back to the fire, his eyes searching the courtyard and finding only the unbroken walls of the buildings around him.

The two men in the shadows moved toward him at a silent move of the hand from the man seated at the fire. Joe backed against the door.

"What's he paying you?" he asked. "What's that fuckin' Loyd paying you?"

They moved toward him silently.

"Tell Loyd I just want to talk to him," Joe said. "That's why I want to find him."

The men moved forward and he could see the long bladed knives they carried, the firelight sent a flicker of silver along the razor edge of the long blades.

Joe snapped his wrist, dropping his butterfly knife into his palm and with a practiced clicking sound, snapped it open in his hand. He held it out in front of him.

"You want to play, motherfucker," he shouted. "Come on, I'll show you who you're fuckin' with here! I'm . . ."

A numbing blow on his arm made him look down to see he was holding out the stump of his wrist. His hand lay on the cobblestones, still gripping his knife.

He was still staring at his hand on the smooth stones when the sound of a heavy blade chopping into his neck brought darkness.

The phone rang in Lonto's bedroom at a quarter to five in the morning. A phone call at a quarter to five is not a good way to start out the day if you're a cop. It is especially not a good way to begin the day if you have already spent half the night worrying about the problems you found as part of the job yesterday. Lonto wanted the phone to stop ringing so he could go back to sleep until seven, which was a more reasonable time to prepare to face the day. He pushed back the covers and picked up the phone.

"Yeah," he said sleepily.

"Tony?"

"None other."

"This is O'Malley. We're over on Silver under the Sixth Street overpass."

"I'm glad for you."

"Sorry about waking you early," O'Malley said. "But you left word you wanted a call if anyone got word on Eddy Loyd or Joe Wells."

"What's going on?" Lonto asked.

"Well, you don't need to look for Joe Wells anymore," O'Malley said. "He's right here, dead as a stone."

"How'd it happen?"

"You won't believe it until you see it."

"I'll be right down."

"Okay, you want me to call Runnion?"

Lonto thought a moment. "No, leave him sleep. With two jobs he needs the rest. I'll fill him in."

Lonto hung up and turned to see Robin watching him sleepily.

"Morning," he said and kissed her.

"Mm," she said. "Feels like the middle of the night."

"It's early. Go back to sleep."

"You have time for something to eat?"

"I'll catch something downtown."

"I wish you'd eat," Robin said. "How can I impress you with my talents in the kitchen if you never have time to eat?"

"You impress me enough with your talents in the bedroom," Lonto said, grinning.

"You're a dirty old man," Robin said, "but I love you anyway."

"Have to go," he said, and kissed her.

"Take a look," O'Malley invited as Lonto walked up.

The body lay face down on the shoulder of the road with the head laying oddly against the right shoulder, a heavy bladed knife was buried deep in the top of the head, almost splitting the skull, its bloody handle standing upright in the police lights.

"What the hell is that?" Lonto asked.

"Looks like a damn sword," Mills said. "You ever seen anything like this, Tony?"

"We get all kinds of shit up here," Lonto said, "but that's no switchblade."

They studied the body. The odd angle of the head was accounted for by the fact that the neck had been almost severed by a blow from the left side, leaving only some skin to hold it attached to the body.

"Someone was sure pissed at him," O'Malley said.

42

"Looks like he was dumped out of a car," Lonto said. "Who found him?"

"Patrol cop. They drive through here about once an hour. Last time through he's laying here with that sword buried in his skull. They say he's Joe the Dog alright, they know him."

"Where they at?"

"Drove down to get some coffee and donuts," O'Malley said. "Nice to have something hot this morning. Where the hell's the medical examiner and his ghouls?"

"Shift change," Lonto said. "It might be a while before they get here."

"Runnion coming?" Mills asked.

"I left word at the desk," Lonto said. "Hope they bring some extra coffee, it's getting cold in the mornings."

"Wait a while," O'Malley said. "It'll be colder than a witch's tit all the time. I hate winter. The only good thing about winter is the garbage in the alleys don't smell so bad."

"Yeah, stays fresher for the rats that way," Mills said. "I seen a rat in one of those apartment buildings on Franklin that was bigger than my cat. Fucker just sat there and showed his teeth at me."

"How do you want to work this, Tony?" O'Malley asked. "You want to take the case, seeing if it ties in with the Loyd thing?"

"If it ties in," Lonto said, "being a supplier seems to be an unhealthy occupation."

"Maybe old Eddy decided to eliminate the competition."

"Here's the M.E.," Mills said. "So, how about it? You taking this one."

"Yeah," Lonto said, "but hang around until the patrolmen get back."

The Lab Unit arrived shortly behind the medical examiner and the patrol cops parked behind them. The scene suddenly became busy, while the detectives drank coffee and waited. Hooley examined the body silently and asked one of the lab technicians to help him turn the body after he removed the heavy knife from the skull to preserve any prints. Once the body had been turned over, they discovered its right hand had been severed at the wrist; and they found the hand had been stuffed into the left pocket of its wearer's jacket, which they thought was considerate of the killer. What was missing was not at all considerate.

Joe's trousers were open, making it obvious he wore no shorts. It was also obvious that someone had used a very sharp knife on him.

O'Malley and Mills exchanged glances.

"They cut his balls off," O'Malley said in surprise.

"They cut everything off," Mills said. "He's better off dead."

Lonto just swore silently.

"What kind of knife was it?" Pat Runnion asked.

"Hooley said it was some kind of machete," Lonto said.

They were back in the squad room, Lonto sitting behind his desk, Runnion sitting on the corner of it, swinging his leg. The morning sun through the windows suggested warmth but it was cold in the room because the newly installed central heating system had the temperature in the building down to a chilly fifty degrees. The building maintenance men were no doubt trying to make up for July when the heating system could only be set to blow warm air around the room. Runnion was a little pissed that Lonto had not called him in early on the case when he had answered the early call. Runnion did not like the idea that his partner did not want him on a case. He rubbed his tired eyes, and wondered if Lonto might be considering a new partner.

"Does cutting his privates off have any particular meaning?" he asked.

"Like what?"

"Like he was screwing around with someone's wife," Runnion said.

"Not that I know of," Lonto said. "They break a guy's legs for that."

"Cut the throat of a snitch, I think," Runnion said. "Or break a guy's arms if he's stealing from them."

"Girl over on Prior cut her husband's balls off with a razor a few years ago," Lonto said. "Caught him in bed with her girlfriend."

"Maybe someone was just making a point when they chopped him up," Runnion said. "He was a dealer, wasn't he?"

"He's tied in with Eddy Loyd somehow. Whatever the hell is going on is tied into the cocaine trade."

"Half the crap that goes on down here is tied into the damn cocaine trade."

"Yeah, and the other half is tied into heroin, speed, downers or booze, not to mention the pot heads." Lonto shrugged, and looked into the in basket on his desk. "Sometimes I wish they'd legalize the crap and let 'em all turn into Lotus Eaters."

"Legalizing heroin didn't work in England," Runnion said.

"Wouldn't here either," Lonto said, looking in his desk drawer. "You pull the file on Joe Wells?"

"It's under the phone there," Runnion said. "According to his jacket he's been arrested eight times, convicted once and did three years at Backwater for cutting up some junkie. Supposed to have been a bad dude with a knife."

"He wasn't bad enough."

"I wonder if he was alive when they cut his nuts off," Runnion said. "I get jumpy just thinking about that."

"I guess it doesn't make a hell of a lot of difference. Hooley will probably tell us though. I still have to go with the idea that it's tied into the cocaine trade. Maybe Loyd figured he would drop a dime on him or something."

"This Loyd sounds like a bad customer," Runnion said.

"He's tough and mean. Smart enough to use the laws to protect his ass, but he's a rapist and a killer in my book. I really hate these big money pushers."

"You sound like there's something personal about this one," Runnion said.

"What Loyd's record doesn't say is the little girl he raped and finally did time for has never been right in the head since then," Lonto said, "and we've got a couple of unsolved murders of young girls that I think are his."

"You two have a minute?" Jaworski asked. They turned simultaneously to find the lieutenant standing there, waiting with another man. The stranger was a tall dark man who looked like a bull fighter, with a narrow waist, wide shoulders and dark, expressionless eyes. He was perhaps thirty-five years old, with a trace of gray in his black hair and a neatly trimmed military mustache. There was a deep scar across his left cheek, reaching up high on the cheekbone. He studied the two men calmly.

"This is Mr. Victor Ruiz," Jaworski said. "He's up from the Miami Narcotics Bureau working a case. Uptown says to give him all the cooperation he needs."

Lonto and Runnion shook hands with Ruiz and introduced themselves.

"Miami, huh?" Lonto said. "What brings you up here?"

"Originally I was with the Federal drug enforcement in Colombia, then Miami," Ruiz said. "I'm working a cocaine case that seems to lead me here."

"You got rid of any accent," Runnion said.

"I went to college at Southwestern in Arizona," Ruiz said. "But English is a second language in our country." His teeth were very even and white when he smiled.

"I'll leave Mr. Ruiz with you," Jaworski said.

As Jaworski walked away, Lonto asked, "What can we do for you, Mr. Ruiz?"

"You can start by calling me Victor," Ruiz said. "The lieutenant tells me you're working on a drug case. Cocaine? He also said you're a couple of the best men he has on the streets."

"The lieutenant said that?" Runnion asked, amazed.

"Grab that chair and sit down," Lonto said, and indicated a chair at the next desk.

Ruiz sat. Looking like a relaxed cat, he crossed his legs and smiled.

"I also understand you have a murder tied into this cocaine case. Is that right?"

Lonto nodded. "One this morning or last night," he said. "Another likely homicide a few days ago."

"The murder this morning," Ruiz said. "Was a very large knife used?"

"A machete, our medical examiner said."

"Actually, I believe it may be what we call a cane knife if the description I heard was correct," Ruiz said. "About twenty-four inches over all with a wood handle and a rather blunt tip."

"That sounds like it," Lonto said. "Is one of these cane knives involved in the case down in Miami?"

"Let's say it's a weapon of preference of the group I'm interested in, but in Miami they were also well armed with pistols and automatic rifles."

"They *were* well armed?" Lonto asked.

"We managed to break up the main group," Ruiz said. "I believe the leader with his people moved up here."

"Are we talking about Colombians, or what?" Lonto asked. "We have a large South American and Mexican population in the city."

"Are you familiar with the name Caribe?" Ruiz asked. He waited, and then went on. "Once they were a people found through much of South America and the Caribbean. They've been exterminated as tribes now, except for those living on the north coast of South America."

"Are they some sort of primitives?" Runnion asked.

"Exposure to both our cultures have moved some of them into the civilized world. They learned quite quickly that the coco leaves they chewed daily had a value to the drug traders and eventually some became drug dealers themselves. The cane knives are a favorite way of eliminating competition in the drug trade when they move into an area. You could meet one of them in your Latin district and not know him from one of us."

Lonto and Runnion exchanged glances.

"They're South American then?" Runnion asked.

"The South American have had a civilization as long as the Europeans have," Ruiz said angrily. "We're not mongrel jungle Indians."

"Well," Lonto said, "except for the murder this morning, there doesn't seem to be any drug war going on here. Nobody is saying anything about any new bunch in the city."

"If you've got their names we can run them through records," Runnion said.

"I have already at your central office," Ruiz said, smiling again. "No records, no match. I would appreciate a chance to share your information on this murder and the drug raid earlier, if you don't mind. And perhaps any records of any murders during the past six months."

"You're that sure this bunch is operating in this city?" Lonto asked.

Ruiz looked past them out the window at the city and was silent a long while. Then he said, "They're out there. I know they're here."

"How do you know?" Runnion asked.

Ruiz smiled. "How do you call it? A feeling in the gut? Anyway, in Miami we traced their drug supply from Colombia. That supply line seems to lead here now."

"Does Lieutenant Jaworski know?" Lonto asked.

"He knows I'm tracing a pipeline," Ruiz said. "Could I see those records now?"

"We'll get them," Lonto said. "You can use that desk in the corner."

Trash Can O'Toole was a man who had operated his business on Silver Street for fifty years. He had watched the street grow from a riverfront red-light district crowded with barge men and traders to a more sophisticated red-light district that offered something to anyone in the city seeking an evening's excitement. On Silver Street, everything was available for a price from high-grade cocaine and five-hundred-dollar call girls to a bag of marijuana for ten dollars and a backseat quickie with a high-school girl just breaking into the trade. You could also get a mickey in your drink, mugged, or murdered, and a dose of any number of venereal diseases. There was always some action going on the street and Trash Can loved the action. His real name was Sean O'Toole but on Silver Street he had been Trash Can ever since the day he appeared on the corner of Fourth and Silver and began selling newspapers he had stashed on the top of an overturned trash can. Even the booth he now sold his newspapers from bore the name Trash Can O'Toole.

Trash Can was sixty-eight but to the people on the street he had always been there. He was small, bald, darkly weathered and wrinkled like an old walnut with bright eyes, yellowing teeth, and a happy smile. He knew more about the red-light district and the people there than anyone. His insight and knowledge of the street did not come from the sale of newspapers alone. The fact that he was the favorite bookie of the district kept him in touch with all the action.

All that inside knowledge of the street made Trash Can a very valuable man to Tony Lonto who checked with him regularly. Lonto was well aware that the main bookie action in the district passed through Trash Can's hands. In fact, if any of the cops at River Station were interested in putting part of their hard-earned paycheck on a game, a fight, or on the nose of a mud runner at the track, they would call on Trash Can, never mind that gambling was illegal in the state. Trash Can always paid off when you won and he never let a bettor get in over his head, and when you are buried daily in murder, rape, robbery, and dope cases, a bit of bookie action does not merit a lot of police attention.

For Lonto, Trash Can would always come through with the information he needed. Lonto did not consider Trash

Can a stoolie, he was in fact an old friend from the days when Lonto was torn between the idea of becoming a thief, a pusher, a pimp like most of the neighborhood punks, or joining the army. After the army, Lonto had joined the force, and Trash Can considered him one of the few successes the district had produced.

Trash Can could always be found at his booth on the corner or in his neat efficiency apartment above the drug store where he wrote dark, bastardized poetry about the people on the street. Today he was at his place of business, talking to a young hooker who had learned that he was one of the few men on the strip she could talk to who was not interested in taking her to bed or running some sort of game. Well, maybe he wasn't completely disinterested in the bed part. Some of the girls said there was still life in the old man, but he was nice to talk to when business was slow.

He nodded in greeting as Lonto and Runnion walked over, and together they watched the girl sway down the street.

Then he sighed.

"If I was twenty years younger I'd take her off the street and get her a place in the country. She's from Kansas, you know?"

"Why not get her a place and retire?" Lonto said, "You'll probably be around twenty years yet."

"I like variety," Trash Can said. "What's on your mind, Tony?"

He sat silently and listened as Lonto talked.

"Eddy Loyd," he said. "Yeah. Used to be pushing nickel and dime bags on the street, now I hear he's a big supplier, like Joe the Dog was."

"You hear anything about where he is?"

"I heard he's got some people looking for him."

"Yeah, us."

"Someone's looking for him beside you," Trash Can said. "Word was Joe the Dog would give up an ounce of coke to find him."

"He must have wanted to find him pretty bad," Runnion said.

"Loyd shouldn't be too hard to find. If he's around somebody will know. What do you want him for?"

"He's got a lot of questions to answer," Lonto said.

"Man to ask questions would be Loyd's boss," Trash Can said. "You're not thinking he's operating alone are you? Like I said, he was nickel and dime crap until someone started supplying him."

"I thought he was an independent."

"Word was that Loyd, Joe, and another guy they call JR all started working for the same guy about the same time."

"This guy have a name?" Runnion asked.

Trash Can reached under the counter and poured himself a cup of coffee from the thermos. "I'm going to get one of those little gas heaters for the booth this year. Jesus, it can get cold around here in the winter. I might even take a vacation down to Miami if I can find someone to run the booth. I never had a vacation. You ever been to Miami, Tony?"

"Once. It's nice," Lonto said. "Have you got anything on this supplier?"

"I can't give you anything on him, Tony. People are real spooky about him. They don't talk on that subject."

"What about Loyd?"

"Loyd they'll talk about. He's a mean son of a bitch but lots of people know him."

"Okay, see what you can find out."

"Sure, if he's still around."

"What do you mean?" Lonto asked. "Loyd's not smart enough to get out of the city, not when he's got a good thing going."

"Last six or seven months there's been more than one pusher around here disappeared suddenly," Trash Can said. "One day they're here, the next they're gone."

"No one's reported anyone missing," Runnion said.

"Who reports a pusher missing?" Trash Can asked. "Junkies just find another pusher."

"Maybe they did leave town," Runnion said.

"The only time a pusher moves is when he goes to jail. These guys are from nowhere. The smart one's the supplier. A street pusher would stay in a burning building if he was selling his shit."

"So what are you saying?"

"Just that maybe this Loyd ain't around," Trash Can said. "But if he is I'll find him. I'll give you a call when I do."

The caretaker at Joe Wells's apartment building on North Sixtieth Street in the Walkers Bluff area was not pleased with all the police attention his building was getting. He had spent the morning answering questions and watching the police act like a demented wrecking crew in Joe Wells's apartment. To make matters worse, today was the day when he was scheduled to steam the rugs in the hall, and the police had managed to put him a half day behind on his weekly schedule, which he wanted to make up this afternoon. What he didn't want this afternoon was more police disrupting his work when he was only the super and not in charge of watching the renters.

"I only take care of the building," he said. "The renters pay their rent to the owner, and I take care of the maintenance. Mr. Wells paid his rent and he never had any problems in his apartment. I don't know him."

"Did he have any visitors here?" Lonto asked.

"Everyone here has visitors. Which ones came to see him I wouldn't know. This is a busy place."

"Why is it so busy?"

"There's just a lot of traffic in this building. Some of the girls here have quite a few male visitors."

"We have to take another look at Wells's apartment," Lonto said.

"I suppose you can't make any more of a mess than they did this morning," the caretaker said, and led them upstairs to unlock the door for them.

The apartment was small and without any personal touch.

A small bedroom, a kitchen, living room, and a bathroom. It did not look like the apartment of a man who was successful enough at pushing cocaine to drive a new car and own the dozen four-hundred-dollar suits still hanging in the closet. In the earlier search the police had stripped the bed leaving the black satin sheets in a pile on the stained mattress.

"You ever slept on silk sheets?" Runnion asked.

"Never had the chance," Lonto said. "Looks like Wells spent his money on cars, clothes, and jewelry. Lab said he was still wearing his watch and rings but there was no sign of his wallet."

"Not likely robbery," Runnion said. "A mugger down there would have picked him clean, right down to his shoes."

"Unless he was carrying a lot of blow and got hit for that," Lonto said. He opened a dresser drawer to sort through the jumble of shirts and socks inside. "Looks like the guys tossed the place pretty good. No cocaine around."

"So maybe we're wasting our time," Runnion said.

They both turned toward the door when someone knocked. Lonto held up his hand and moved quietly to the door.

"Yeah?" he said. "Who is it?"

"Come on, Joe," the voice said. "Open up. I got money."

"How much?" Lonto asked, grinning at Runnion.

"I got enough. I turned a trick," the voice said.

Lonto waited.

"Come on! I really need some, Joe."

Lonto opened the door, expecting a well-worn street hooker wanting to trade a half hour of her services for enough dope to let her face a hard day's work on the strip. The young girl standing in the hall studied Lonto with big eyes and said, "You're not Joe."

She looked past him into the apartment as though expecting her pusher to appear, then she frowned. She was perhaps five four or five five, with coppery red hair, green eyes, and a spray of freckles across her nose. She was wearing a bulky white sweater and jeans. A blue bookbag hung from her right shoulder. Lonto estimated she was fourteen or fifteen years old.

"Who are you?" she asked. "Is Joe here?"

"Not right now," Lonto said.

"Where's he at?" she asked, and glanced at Runnion standing to the left of the door. She raised her eyebrows.

"What's going on?" she asked. She glanced down the hall toward the stairway.

"We're the police," Lonto said, taking his badge case from his pocket and holding it so she could read the ID card.

"Oh shit!" she said.

"Would you step in here and tell us who you are please?" Lonto asked, holding the door open.

"I'll be late for class," she said, and moved into the apartment. Her eyes nervously searched the stripped apartment. She obviously knew something was wrong now. "Wow, what happened?"

"How about a name," Lonto said.

"Kimberly Harris. Was there a burglary?"

"When did you last see Joe Wells, Miss Harris?" Lonto asked.

"Yesterday afternoon," she said. "I suppose I'm in trouble, huh?"

"Did you buy cocaine from Wells yesterday?" Runnion asked.

"No."

"Why not? He's your pusher isn't he?"

She shrugged.

"How old are you?" Lonto asked. "We'd like to see some ID."

"I'm sixteen," she said. "I don't have an ID." Lonto glanced at Runnion. A high-school kid turning tricks for dope while she goes to school, he thought. He'd seen them picked up for prostitution at twelve.

"Was Wells supposed to meet you here today?" Lonto asked.

"He's usually here."

"You turn tricks on your lunch hour for dope money?" Runnion asked, getting tough.

Anger showed in her eyes. She hesitated a moment. "You're not going to arrest me, are you? My dad will kill me."

"Somebody already killed Joe Wells," Runnion said, bluntly.

"Come on!" Kimberly said. "He was just here yesterday."

"He was found murdered early this morning," Lonto said.

She suddenly became a very scared young girl, surprise and shock showing in her eyes.

"I don't really know anything about Joe," she said. "I only see him once or sometimes twice a week."

"How long have you been buying crack from him?" Runnion asked.

"Since this spring."

"Is he your pimp, too?" Runnion asked.

She suddenly burst into tears. Lonto and Runnion watched her, feeling uncomfortable and awkward. She fumbled in her bookbag for a tissue, wiped her eyes. "I'm not a whore," she whispered.

"You're turning tricks for dope money," Runnion said angrily. "What do you call it?"

"Take it easy, Pat," Lonto said, "she's just a kid."

"Did Wells suggest you turn some tricks for your money?" Lonto asked the girl.

She nodded. "He sent me to see a friend of his. She was actually married to him once. Said she would show me how to make some easy money during my lunch hour."

"What's this friend's name?"

"Windy Sterling," she said. "But I don't think that's her real name. I have her phone number."

"Does she arrange your dates for you?" Lonto asked.

"I only did it once or twice a month," she said, and began crying again. "It was always nice guys who work uptown who wanted a date at lunch time."

"Where does this Sterling woman live?" Lonto asked.

"Seventy-Seven-Sixteen Cedar Street East," the girl said. "It's in Maple Hills." She blew her nose, looked for a place to put the tissue and finally kept it in her hand while she looked in her bag for another.

"Do you know any of the other customers that came here?"

"I've seen a couple in the hall," she said, "you know, like they were just leaving. But I don't know them."

"What time did you see Wells yesterday?" Lonto asked.

"It must have been about three-thirty, right after school. I stopped before I caught my bus home."

"Was he alone then?"

"I don't know," she said. "He wouldn't let me in when he found out I didn't have any money."

"And that's the last time you saw him?"

"Yeah. Is he really dead?" Kimberly asked. "Are you going to arrest me or something?"

Lonto hesitated a moment, and then said, "I don't think that's necessary right now. But what we are going to do is call a policewoman down here, and she's going to take you down to the River Station where your parents can come and get you after you've looked at some mugshot books."

"Oh, shit," the girl said.

4

It was going to be one of those nights.

The unmarked radio car O'Malley was driving was number thirteen on the motor pool's roster and perversely lived up to its unlucky listing. That summer, number thirteen had repeatedly been in the shop for radio repair, a new transmission, and an unknown electrical problem, which none of the swearing mechanics had been able to identify. Instead, after the movie had appeared in the city, the mechanics began to refer to car thirteen as having gremlins. Tonight, a flat tire was its contribution to its growing gremlin personality, which was made worse by the fact that it was only three years old.

The first call had been received by the desk sergeant at the River Station at eleven forty-five. A robbery-with-shots-fired call that had resulted in two patrol cars sent to the scene. The patrolmen were not at all surprised to find the street empty of any likely robbery suspect and a corpse lying behind the counter of the small grocery store. In the Rice Street section of the city, the results of a police car's siren responding to a call was to clear the streets more effectively than a tornado warning.

O'Malley and Mills, who were working the eleven-to-seven shift that month, had already answered a call on a knifing in a bar on Seventh Avenue only to find the bar empty when they arrived. The second call, along with the flat tire was waiting when they returned to the car.

Neither man was in a cheerful mood when they arrived at the scene a half hour late. The patrolman who had first responded to the call was none too pleased with the late arrival of the detectives either, but realized that rank has its benefits. He recognized O'Malley and Mills as they parked illegally and walked into the store.

"What have you got?" O'Malley asked the patrolman.

"Looks like a robbery murder. My partner's with the guy's sister and father by the window there. Body's behind the counter. Sister came in to help close the place and found the brother dead, cash register empty."

The two detectives walked around the counter to look at the body. The assistant medical examiner was studying the body, pointing out items of interest for the photographer to shoot. The body lay face down on the worn linoleum, a dark puddle of blood had collected under the head. The cash register was open and empty except for some change. On the floor about two feet from the body was an open green metal box, its contents scattered behind the counter: personal checks and food stamps.

O'Malley knelt at the counter and pointed. "You get a picture of this?" he asked.

"What?"

"Cartridge case, small caliber."

"Looks like a twenty-five caliber," Mills said.

"Yeah, we got that," the photographer said and kept snapping pictures.

"How about it, doc? You about finished?"

"Few more minutes." He wiped his face with a handkerchief. "What took you guys so long tonight?"

"We got that damn car thirteen," Mills said.

"That one, huh!" He made a final examination of the body. "I'm through."

O'Malley and Mills waited expectantly.

"He was shot once in the face. Slug entered upward through the bridge of the nose, exited through the back of the skull at an upward angle. Death was likely instantaneous."

"How about time?"

"Give me a break, guys. Less than an hour ago for sure, but it's warm in here so the body might have been here awhile before the girl found him." He snapped shut his bag. "You guys might have a killer here who likes to sign his jobs though."

"Let's have it," O'Malley said, waiting.

"Who ever shot him took the time to cut off his right ear. Clean job, close to the skull with a sharp knife or razor."

"Anybody find the ear?" O'Malley asked.

"Nope." The assistant M.E. checked his watch. "I'm out of here," he said.

"I knew it was going to be one of those nights when we got that car," Mills said. "I've been checking. Every time we do a shift in thirteen we get at least ten more calls. Nothin' goes right when we get that damn car."

"I just hope this isn't another one like the wig murderer they had uptown. He used to rape and murder his victims and leave them wearing a blonde wig. Took a while to catch that bastard," O'Malley said.

"So what happened to him?"

"He's upstate at the funny farm," O'Malley said. "Doctors said he was killing his prostitute mother over and over again." He sighed. "Let's go talk to the family."

The family was a tall, dark-haired girl about fifteen and a white-haired old man who might have been anywhere from sixty to a hundred years old. The old man's long white hair framed a dark, wrinkled face and dark eyes that glared brightly at the world.

"I'm Detective O'Malley," O'Malley said, "River Station. I'm sorry, sir, but we have to ask some questions."

"No hablo ingles," the old man said.

"Oh, hell," O'Malley said. "Have we got anyone here who speaks Spanish?"

"My father has not learned English," the girl said. "I will translate for him." Her voice was low and throaty, almost seductive.

"Can you give us your brother's name, please?"

"Anthony Galeas."
"And yours?"
"Arcadia Galeas," she said. "My father's name is Tino."
"I understand you found your brother?"
The girl nodded.
"What time was that, Miss Galeas?"
"It was at eleven-thirty when I came."
"And you called the police right away?"
Again she nodded.
"You were coming in to help him close for the night?"
"Yes."
"Do you live near here?"
"Above this store," she said. "I come down the stairs over there and find him."
"You live directly above the store and didn't hear anything? No loud voices, no shots fired?"
She shook her head. "There was no shot or I would have heard."
"When you came downstairs was anyone in the store?"
"No one."
"Did you touch the body, or move it?"
"I only call the police."
"Did your father hear anything?"
O'Malley watched as she talked rapidly to the old man who stared at them angrily and answered in one brief sentence. His voice was surprisingly strong.
"He heard nothing," the girl said. "There was no shot fired or he would hear."
"What time did you leave the store?"
"I go up at nine," she said.
"Just one more thing, Miss Galeas. Did your brother have any enemies here in the neighborhood?"
"Enemies?"
"Anyone who was angry at your brother? Did he have any trouble with any of the neighbors? We'll need a list of people he knew."

"There is no one he knew outside the family. In our country only the family is important."

O'Malley asked the patrolman standing nearby to take the girl and the old man upstairs, and then as the lab boys were finishing, he examined the brass cartridge case now in a plastic evidence bag and requested that they spend what time was needed to locate the spent slug. Arcadia Galeas had told him neither she nor her father had heard a shot. With the slug, the lab could possibly tell if a silencer had been used on the gun.

It was almost three in the morning when the body was on its way to the morgue and the lab technicians were finished. They had talked to the other tenants in the building and were met with the same silent dark faces of people who did not trust the police. They had learned only that Anthony Galeas was the son of Tino and had no friends outside the family.

"Talkative bunch aren't they?" Mills said, when they finished. "There must be twenty men in this building and maybe eight women. I didn't see any kids did you?"

"Maybe they were sleeping," O'Malley said.

"That girl was pretty cool about it too," Mills went on. "Not a tear over her brother, like she'd seen it all before."

"People show their grief in different ways," O'Malley said. "Let's call in and get something to eat before we go in."

When they reached the car, they found that the radio was dead once more.

Detective Carl Pavolny was also working the graveyard shift that night. For a cop on the street working on his own personal cocaine business with one of his few remaining pushers, nighttime is the prudent time to be on the streets. For many people the night is the time for partying and lovers. When the day is over they head for the bars and bright lights or maybe enjoy a quiet evening at home with the family. Pavolny and John Richards were not interested in bright lights or lovers. John Richards, who was called JR on the street, had remembered that Eddy Loyd did have a regular girlfriend, at least he had a woman who he visited at those times when he was not looking for schoolgirls in the local parks. Actually, they had been unable to locate Eddy Loyd in any of his usual haunts and thought his sometimes girlfriend just might have an idea where he was at. If you're a badge carrying member of the city's finest, two in the morning is a reasonable time to go visiting.

For Connie Samuel, a knock on the door at two in the morning could only mean one of two things. It was either the cops coming around to bust her once more for prostitution, or it was one of her regular customers who wanted a quickie after his date for the night had decided to keep her legs crossed. Either way, both choices were an accepted part of her business.

From behind the door, Connie asked, "Who is it?"

"Police," Pavolny said.

"Now what? At two A.M.?"

"Open the door, Samuel."

"What's this about?"

"We want to ask you some questions," Pavolny said. "You want us to kick it down?"

They heard the door bar scrape and the lock click, then a doorchain being slid into place. The door opened a crack.

"Let's see some identification," Connie said.

Pavolny held his badge and ID case up. "Come on," he said. "You can stop stalling now."

"Is this a bust?"

"We want to ask you some questions about Eddy Loyd."

"Eddy?"

"Yeah, your sometimes boyfriend. Now open up."

"Eddy Loyd?" Connie said again. She had not seen Eddy for more than a month now. It was Eddy who sometimes gave her cocaine to sell to her customers. Jesus, did Eddy get busted and tell the cops she was pushing? The dirty perverted bastard would do something like that.

"Eddy hasn't been around here for a month," Connie said. "The bastard don't tell me nothing when he is around."

"We still want to ask some questions."

"Okay, okay, but make it fast will you? I'm a working girl."

She slid the safety chain and opened the door wide.

They walked into the apartment. They were in a living room, kitchen combination; a door opened into a small bedroom off to the right. Next to the stove was a table with two chairs. There were a couch and easy chair flanking a low coffee table. The apartment was clean, with a tablecloth on the painted table and several small figurines around the room. There was a tall vase with brightly colored paper flowers on the coffee table.

"Check the bedroom," Pavolny said. He pointed to the couch. "Sit down."

"What do you want Eddy for now?" Connie asked. She was watching them carefully, wondering if they were going to take her down to the station.

"When's the last time you seen him?" Pavolny said.

"I told you. He hasn't been around for more than a month."

"The bitch is lying," JR said. "She wouldn't tell a cop anything. Let me at her for about ten minutes, I'll make her talk."

Connie watched him walk toward her across the room, and sat there in surprise as he casually knocked her over on the couch with an open-handed slap. JR was not interested if she would tell them the truth because of her fear of authority, that was a theory the cops worked on. His theory was that people would talk to avoid pain.

Connie was touching the side of her face gently, thinking

she would probably get a bruise or a black eye. JR grabbed her by the hair to pull her upright on the couch.

"Sit up, bitch," he said. "You ain't hurt."

Connie was crying.

"Stop your bawling. You ain't hurt yet."

After being knocked over on the couch and feeling her face beginning to swell, Connie disagreed completely with that. She was also thinking that she had made a bad mistake and these two were maybe not cops. Now they were in her apartment and she didn't know what they wanted. It wasn't that she hadn't been hit by a cop before. It was just that the one who had hit her didn't seem like any cop to her.

"What do you want?" Connie said.

"A little cooperation," Pavolny said. "We want to know where Eddy's holed up at."

"I told you I don't have any idea where that bastard is at. He hangs around here once in a while."

"And you sell coke for him, don't you?" Pavolny said. "You supply your tricks with a little blow after they get laid."

"Coke? What are you talking about? I don't sell any coke. I don't know what you're talking about."

"Hit her," Pavolny said. "Help her remember."

The blow came quickly before she could turn her head. JR's fist smashed into her nose and she heard the bones break. She sat there dazed watching the blood pour down her face and robe.

She stared at them in amazement. She knew they couldn't be cops now. Cops don't break bones, cops don't want to leave marks when they hit you. These two would leave all the marks and broken bones they wanted. But she didn't know what they wanted.

"I don't know anything about Eddy."

She kept staring at them and trying to make her nose stop bleeding. She would tell them anything they wanted to know, but she didn't know what they wanted.

Pavolny sat down in the easy chair and crossed his legs. "Make her talk," he said to JR.

The squad room was relatively quiet when Lonto arrived in the morning, but then it was only seven, and the city had not gotten into the full swing of the day's activities. The graveyard-shift men were still at their desks, laboriously typing up their reports, while the relieving shift drank coffee and exchanged stories on the night's bookings that might apply to the coming day's events.

The relieving detectives were Lonto, Runnion, Vincent Gonzalez, and David Washington. Gonzalez and Washington did not get through their first cup of coffee before they had to answer a call on a robbery taking place on the crosstown bus. Lonto and Runnion were at their desks, reading the last night's bookings, and drinking bitter coffee left over from the graveyard shift when Victor Ruiz arrived.

"I will need to examine the files once more," Ruiz said.

Lonto glanced up to see he was wearing faded jeans pulled down over an old pair of engineer boots, a black T-shirt, and an old, short Levi jacket with a hole in the elbow of the right sleeve. A small gold earring was fixed on his left ear and a gold chain hung around his neck. In contrast to the well-dressed professional look he had first presented, his appearance today was grimy and tattered, and his once neatly trimmed mustache appeared unkempt, matching his unshaven jaw.

"Been checking out the streets?" Lonto asked.

Ruiz grinned and approached the desk. "One needs to fit in with the local environment," he said. "In Miami you have to walk the walk and talk the talk to get any information."

"Any luck so far?" Lonto asked, leaning back in the chair.

Ruiz looked directly into his eyes and shook his head slightly. This one is one to be careful with, he thought, a dangerous man who will not trust easily, with the relaxed air of the big cat, like he'd always be waiting for a man to make a small mistake, or one detail not to fit a pattern. Lonto was thinking there was a lot about this man they didn't know. He did not like the idea of an outsider working the streets in their precinct.

"Want some of this?" Runnion asked, nodding at the cup in his hand. "One cup will give you a whole new view of coffee."

A good team here, Ruiz thought. The big one with the coffee was without the experience yet, more willing to trust perhaps, but not one to relax too much with. Even the lieutenant who was in charge must be watched, but he had the responsibility of command and would accept his superiors instructions to cooperate.

"How is the progress on the murder of this Wells man?" Ruiz asked.

"Slow. We should get the lab reports today," Lonto said. "We tracked a woman he worked with at least."

"I'll get the coffee," Runnion said. "You want any more, Tony?"

"I'm cured of that batch for the morning," Lonto said.

Runnion headed across the room to the table below the bulletin board where the battered coffee urn sat.

"This woman? She in the cocaine business also?" Ruiz asked.

"Maybe there's a drug connection, but right now I'd guess she's pushing call girls."

"A *puta?*"

"She runs an on-call whore house. You call her and she sends a girl over. They call them an escort service or massage service I guess."

Ruiz shrugged. "In my country a *puta* only needs a license with a doctor's certificate. It is a small matter. How would Wells be connected with her?"

"Most of our crime is connected with the drug trade in one way or the other. Have you got any leads on the group— these Caribes you're looking for?"

"They are secretive people," Ruiz said, "but someone

will know where they are. They need to go outside their group to market the cocaine."

"I don't think they could operate here without our hearing of it," Lonto said. "Unless their organization is very good."

"They are very good," Ruiz said.

"Here you go," Runnion said, returning with the coffee. "There does seem to be more cocaine on the street lately. More than the usual supply."

"Maybe an unusual increase would show up in the number of addict busts lately," Lonto suggested. "Booking sheets over the past few months might show that."

"No need," Ruiz said. "I am sure they are here. After I've gone over the files I would like to join you for a day or so on the street. Your knowledge of the people will help me."

He did not like the idea of Lonto taking too much interest in his case. Not when I have already located them, he thought. Better to stay close to these two if they need to be directed elsewhere.

"Okay with me," Lonto said. "Clear it with the lieutenant and we'll give you a visitor's tour of the local hot spots."

"Can I use the same desk today?" Ruiz asked.

"Might as well," Lonto said, glancing at his watch. "We've got an early appointment with a madam who's not expecting us."

"You are right," Ruiz said, looking at his paper cup in distaste. "I did not believe coffee could result in this."

Erma Perkins, or Windy Sterling as she was listed on the occupants register at the desk, was not a late sleeper. She had already spent an hour in the exercise room on the sixth floor when she returned to her apartment to find two detectives waiting outside her door. She was wearing a black, skintight exercise suit that would violate every dress code in the book. She was wet with sweat, and Lonto wondered why he always found a sweating woman exciting. She said, "You look like cops," and then took her door key from the pocket of a black sweatband on her wrist.

"And you've had your share of experience with cops, right, Miss Sterling?" Lonto asked.

"More than enough," Windy said, and opened the door of her apartment. She gestured toward the living room. All three sat down around a low, glass-top coffee table.

"What's this about?" Windy finally asked.

"First we'd like to ask you some questions about Joe Wells," Lonto said. "I understand that you were married to him once."

"I was wondering when you'd get around to me," Windy said. "I read about it in the paper."

"When's the last time you saw him?"

"A few weeks ago," Windy said. "He called me."

"Does that mean you never saw him, just talked to him over the phone?"

"I haven't actually seen him in nearly three months. He fools around in some heavy shit and I don't need that kind of trouble."

"Exactly what was he in to that was heavy?" Lonto asked.

"Don't you guys read the paper? He was into cocaine heavy. I don't want any part of drugs."

"When you talked to him last, did he mention any problems he was having?"

"No. He was always a macho bastard, like he was Superman or something."

"Who were the people he worked with?"

"Are you crazy?" Windy asked. "I don't know any of those people and I don't want to know who they are."

"Would he have mentioned any friends to you?"

"Not likely. We kept in touch but we weren't close. Shit we never were close, even when we were married."

"Did he ever talk about anyone with you?"

"No, he didn't," Windy said. "Wait, he did talk about one guy. Some guy called Freddy or something, maybe it was Eddy, something about this guy raped a cousin of his."

"This guy have a last name?"

"He never said."

"That the only person he mentioned?"

She smiled. "We didn't do a lot of talking when we were together," she said. "I only remember that one because he was really pissed off."

"You run an escort service from this apartment?" Lonto asked. "Or do you call it a massage service?"

She was silent a moment. "I knew this would turn into a third degree sooner or later," she said.

"This isn't a third degree," Lonto said. "We know you operate an escort service that provides call girls."

"What the girls do on their dates is their own business," Windy said. "I just provide girls as escorts."

"Sure you do," Runnion said. "You even provide sixteen-year-old schoolgirls."

"My girls are all eighteen or over," Windy said. "What is this anyway? You came here to talk about Joe."

"We don't seem to be getting any cooperation with the names of his associates," Lonto said.

"We can still get her on running her business with the minor," Runnion said. "She'll do a couple of years on that."

"Hey! Wait a minute," Windy said. "You guys can't do that. I don't know who Joe's friends are now if he has any. We haven't been living together for more than a year."

"Her memory will improve after a few days in a cell," Runnion said, looking around the apartment. "It won't be as comfortable as this though."

"But I don't know!"

"This is a murder we're investigating. We can charge you with forcing a minor into prostitution and subpoena you before a grand jury on the murder while you're in jail. A judge could be real unhappy with you by the time you got to court for sentencing."

"You can't do that," she said.

"Yes we can," Runnion said, "and we will if you don't cooperate."

"I don't believe this," she said.

"Believe it."

"You cops are all alike, big gestapo bastards."

They waited.

"If you don't want a free fuck, you want a payoff," Windy said.

"Why don't you get dressed," Lonto said, "we're going downtown."

"Let's go," Runnion said.

"Wait a minute," Windy said.

They waited.

"I really don't know who his friends are now, but I know what the guy was who put him into the coke business."

"What guy?" Lonto asked.

"You won't believe me anyway," Windy said. "He was a cop, a detective like you two."

"How do you know he was a cop?" Lonto asked.

"Oh come on," Windy said. "I was turning tricks on my own then. First time he came by was for a freebie, he had a badge. After that he came around regular. Besides the other girls said he was a narc who liked his free pussy."

"This cop have a name?" Lonto asked.

"She's lying," Runnion said angrily.

"Like I said, you won't believe me," Windy said. "You cops all cover for each other." She looked at Runnion. "I suppose you don't think cops take payoffs, or a free screw either, huh?"

"How about a name?" Lonto said.

"Look, I don't know the names of most of the guys I screw. Why should he be any different? A free lay for a cop is part of the business. One of the girls said this one was into some heavy coke business so I asked him to give Joe a job; that was just before we got a divorce. Next thing I know, Joe's a big-time pusher on the street." She shrugged. "I should have stayed with him a little longer and got some money. He lived off me long enough."

"You say this cop worked narcotics?" Lonto asked.

"That's what he said," Windy nodded. "He wasn't from your precinct though, I know most of the guys from there."

"This cop still visit you?" Lonto asked.

Windy shook her head. "Not since I moved," she said. "I haven't seen him in six months."

"What's the girl's name who told you this cop was into coke?" Lonto asked.

"She called herself Princess on the street," Windy said. "I don't know what her real name was."

"Where does she work?"

"She worked the parlor on Seventh Street, The Soft Touch, for awhile, but she went freelance on the Strip after that. Last I knew she moved uptown to work the convention center and hotels."

"I want you to find her for us, Windy," Lonto said. "Make some calls and let us know when you do."

"Why should I?"

"One good reason is to stay out of jail," Lonto said. "You find Princess for us and we forget all about the minor. That is, if you're telling us the truth."

"You guys never quit do you?" Windy asked.

When Lonto and Runnion returned to the squad room that afternoon there were two items waiting on Lonto's desk. One was an envelope containing the lab report on Joe Wells. The second was a note, a request that Lonto call Detective Hooley at the lab. Lonto opened the lab report and autopsy first.

"What's that?" Runnion asked.

"Autopsy report."

"So what does it get us?"

"Let's see," Lonto said, pulling the papers from the envelope.

"Says Wells was killed by having his neck severed," Lonto said. "Burying that knife in his skull was done after he was dead."

"How about his hand and his nuts?"

Lonto studied the report. "The castration was after he was dead, too. They're not sure about the hand."

"Crap, what does that get us?" Runnion said.

"Nothing," Lonto said. "At least not yet."

"Anything else in there?"

Lonto studied a second piece of paper from the envelope. "Looks like a lab report on the Loyd case too."

"Anything there?"

"Some," Lonto said. "I'm always amazed what the lab can do with blood and hair. We got a blood type of O, which isn't a hell of a lot of help since half the people around have that, but one of the hair samples from the bed was from a young person, probably around fifteen years of age with black hair."

"How do they figure it was a girl?" Runnion asked.

"The hair was saturated with a hair preparation made for women and it was close to eighteen inches long. Lab's best guess, it's a woman. The second sample was blond and short, and from a man. Loyd was blond, so the lab figures it was his."

"So we're looking for a missing girl, black hair, around fifteen," Runnion said. "We can run it through the latest missing persons list."

"Yeah, call it in, maybe we'll get lucky," Lonto said. "I got to call Hooley. By the way, why don't you come home for supper with me? Robin will be glad to see you."

"Can't," Runnion said. "Have to work the other job."

"How's it going?"

"It's okay. What the hell, it has to be. I need the money."

Thoughtfully, Lonto watched him walk away, and reached for the phone on his desk. As he dialed, he nodded at Ruiz still studying records at the end desk.

The phone was answered on the third ring.

"Police Lab."

"That you, Hooley?" Lonto asked.

"None other," Hooley said.

"This is Lonto. What have you got for us?"

"On what?" Hooley asked, angrily. "We're working on more than one case over here."

"I got a note to call you," Lonto said. "Either the Loyd or the Wells case, I suppose. What else you working on for us?"

"Oh, we got that shooting that O'Malley handled, too. You guys are keeping us busy with bodies lately."

"Never a dull moment on River Street," Lonto said. "So what did you want?"

"I hate to take you away from your busy schedule," Hooley said. "I know you'd rather be out playing Dick Tracy than talking to us common lab people. You guys are always in a hurry."

"We do have our moments," Lonto said.

"Anyway, we finally got the reports back on the murder weapon in the Wells case. It's a type of machete called a corn or cane knife. Blade twenty-four inches long with a wooden handle," Hooley said.

"Anything unusual about it?"

"Not a thing," Hooley said. "They're easily obtainable, used as a field knife on farms, forest service, places like that. Cost about seven bucks."

"That's what you wanted to tell me?"

"No, what I wanted to tell you about was the fingerprints we lifted from the blade and handle. Nice clear, easily identified fingerprints. We even ran them for you and got a positive identification to make things easier."

"And?" Lonto asked.

"You'll have to catch him on your own, of course," Hooley went on. "After we did all the detective work you guys get all the glory."

"Damn it, Hooley."

"Okay, the prints on the knife belong to one Eddy Loyd, Tony. Looks like he's your killer."

"So the two cases *are* tied together," Lonto said. "At least now we can tie Loyd into one murder for sure. Anything else?"

"Well, we found traces of cocaine on Wells's clothing but you already knew he was a pusher."

"Okay, thanks, Hooley."

"You going to see O'Malley today?"

"More than likely," Lonto said. "Want him to call you?"

"No. I'm out of here in a minute. Just tell him that shell case he found at the Galeas murder was three-eighty caliber and made in Brazil. Maybe it will help."

"Okay," Lonto said, and hung up.

Smiling, Lonto crossed the room to where Victor Ruiz was stacking the pile of records on his desk.

"Finished?" Lonto asked.

"For the day," Ruiz said. "The lieutenant agreed I should accompany you and your partner for a few days. I will join another team also."

"Okay with me," Lonto said. "Our shift starts at seven-thirty in the morning. You can join us anytime."

"I will be early," Ruiz said. "Have you made progress in the murder of Wells?"

"Some. You can take that one off the list as being connected with these people you're looking for," Lonto said. "Caribes, or whatever you call them. The fingerprints on the murder weapon are a local boy's, Eddy Loyd. Looks like he's our killer. At least our prime suspect for now."

Ruiz nodded, silent as Lonto walked away.

5

Lonto was still tired at breakfast the next morning. He hated cases where bodies led to more bodies in a grim chain, and he felt inadequate to stop the murders before they had run their bloody course. It was like the frustration they faced with a serial killer and knew that a certain number of people would have to die before the killer made enough mistakes to enable the detectives to gain enough knowledge about his method of operation to catch him. The present murders would be solved, he thought, but only after more legwork was done, or they somehow got a break in the case.

So far, the legwork they'd done had brought them only the information that there was maybe a crooked cop involved with Joe Wells. Was it true? And if it was, how did this cop fit in with Loyd? A break there if they could find the hooker called Princess. Could they?

To hell with a crooked cop, he thought. I don't owe a cop a thing once he crosses that line. But what if Runnion has crossed that line, too? Not because he's crooked, but because he needs the money for hospital bills? What do I owe my own partner if he's stepped over that line just a bit?

Lonto shook his head. To hell with that, too, he thought. I'm home. A man should be able to forget his damn work at home and relax with his wife.

"Something wrong with those eggs?" Robin asked, worried.

"Sorry," Lonto said, looking up. "The eggs are fine. I've had my mind on other things."

"So I've noticed. You're getting rings under your eyes too from not sleeping."

"That bad, huh?"

She smiled. "How about some more coffee," she asked.

Robin was seated at the kitchen table across from him. She wore a loose white robe. She was barefoot as usual in the house, and the robe fell open a moment as she rose, offering a brief view of her breast. He watched her silently, wondering why he would be thinking of a case when he was near Robin. He slipped an arm around her hip as she poured the coffee.

"Just what do you have on your mind, mister?" she asked, bumping her hip against him.

"What time is it?"

She smiled. "Forget it, you'd be late for work."

"Guy at work says he never passes up an opportunity because he might never be able to catch up."

"I'll catch you up tonight," she said. "Eat your eggs."

He finished the eggs and sat back with his coffee.

"Tough case, huh?"

"We're getting information, but we're not getting any closer to finding the suspect."

"You'll find him," she assured him.

"Maybe. What bothers me is he's a known felon and not one of our snitches can come up with anything on him. We don't have an idea where he might be holed up."

"It's a big city, you know."

"I suppose. What'd you do yesterday?"

"Didn't I tell you? I went out to the hospital to see Lin."

"How's she doing?"

"Better," Robin said. "At least she's not so worried about money now that Pat got the loan from the police union."

"Union?"

"The union's retirement fund," Robin said. "Didn't he tell you?"

"Yeah," he said. "Forgot for a moment."

"Lin's more relaxed now," Robin said. "Best news is she's at the top of the list now for a transplant and won't have to wait much longer."

"That's good news," Lonto said, glancing at his watch. "I'd better get going or I'll be late."

"Try to get home early, will you?" Robin said. "You need more rest."

"I'll do my best," Lonto said, and kissed her briefly.

Outside the apartment, he swore, softly. Union retirement fund, he thought. The damn union doesn't *have* a retirement fund! Not one a cop can get a loan from.

Mike Reid did not like to drive through the old town business district on the north side of the city. He liked it even less that he had to work there, bulldozing demolished buildings into piles to be loaded onto trucks to make room for new development in the area. The truth of the matter was that the city north of Davis Drive was no place to screw around in. He knew from personal experience that all sorts of things could happen to a guy who crossed Davis looking for a little action. Three years ago, he had been given a mickey, rolled for his paycheck, had his car stolen—all in one night. To make matters worse he had come down with a case of clap, for which his wife had promptly left him. There were lots of guys on the construction crew who had shit happen to them in this part of the city. After his last experience on River Street he had made himself a promise that he would never look for any kind of action north of Davis. Better yet, he would never visit the north side for any purpose.

So where was he working now? The north side, that's where. The way Reid figured it you weren't safe even working on the north side at any time of the day. He didn't feel safe even though after a month on the job nothing had happened. Not even the night watchman at the demolition site had been bothered, but he did report lights in some of the deserted buildings. Reid could imagine all sorts of weird things going on at night in those buildings. The rest of the crew were scattered over a two-block area of the six-block construction site in Old Town that had been condemned by the city and scheduled for redevelopment as low-rent housing. In reality, the city council had realized that without housing available on the north side, the city's poor were slowly moving out into the more affluent neighborhoods by a cooperative process. Since one family couldn't afford the rent, two families moved into a one-family unit and shared the rent. It came as an unpleasant surprise to apartment owners to discover eight to twelve residents living in the one-bedroom unit they had just rented to a couple.

Unpleasant surprises had a way of translating into angry phone calls to city hall and angry phone calls had a way of further translating into fewer votes at the next elections, which could result in the city council members no longer having high-paying jobs, which allowed them to spend several months of the year on business trips in such places as Miami or California and once a year jaunts to Hawaii. The end result was that the mayor and council members suddenly saw the wisdom and the publicity value of turning a six-block area of the north side into a brand-new low-rent district for the poor. In truth the plans and funds for the project had been made available four years ago but the city council had agreed to use the funds for a new convention center downtown at that time.

Mike Reid did not care what sequence of events had led up to the crew spending the next four years working on the north side, nor did he care that the contractor he worked for had bid the job so low that they would spend the following years putting up apartment buildings that would be unfit to live in before they were ten years old. What he did care about was that he had to work down here. The very thought of what could happen to a man around here was something that was likely to give him ulcers before the job was finished.

It didn't seem to bother the rest of the crew, they kept their hard hats on, shoved a heavy wrench in their pocket and piled into their cars at quitting time to head for River Street as if they didn't know what could happen to you down there. After work, all Reid wanted to do was get back to his apartment in Apple Grove, and feel safe until work the next morning.

The day was warm for November.

Reid backed the bulldozer he was operating and viewed the rubble pile in front of him. The excavation was down to basement level, and one more pile would clean the first site. He realized that the strong smell that hung over the area all day seemed to be coming from that collapsed part of the cellar. In this neighborhood the people didn't put dead pets in the garbage, they left them in vacant buildings. The smell gave Reid the creeps. He was willing to bet that there were hundreds of dead things rotting in these buildings. He moved the bulldozer forward and watched the ten-foot blade tear away the final crumbling wall. As the slab fell away, the rotting oily odor rolled over him like a wave, making him gasp and gag as he stared through the safety screen in front of him.

What Reid saw was a headless upper trunk of a body in the rubble. There were other white mounds of rotting meat in the settling dust that also appeared to be bodies laying there in the clear fall sunlight.

Reid heaved his dinner up and stumbled from the dozer. He did not want to be the one to find any bodies, he did not want to even be down here. He wiped his face and stumbled away from the dozer toward the construction shack. He *knew* something like this would happen down here.

"I've seen pictures of things like this in Poland after the Germans were done," Dunlevy said. "Looks like two, three people there."

He was holding a handkerchief over his nose and staring at the bodies in the rubble. Phillips, his partner, was looking too, covering his nose with a handkerchief. They had arrived first on the scene since, on paper, the Highland Park Station shared the policing of the Old Town district with River Station, the theory being that a joint coverage of a high-crime area would provide more police protection. In reality, the Highland Park Station had a crime rate that was equal to, or worse than, River Station and they shared very few of the cases with them except through making appearances at joint drug busts and homicides. The bodies in the rubble were clearly homicides.

"You see any heads?" Phillips asked. "Looks like a slaughterhouse."

"Looks like someone's been dumping them here for quite awhile," Dunlevy observed. "Arms and legs cut off, too."

The two men were wearing neat, gray business suits and backed quickly away from the rubble when a fitful breeze coiled the ripe odor around them.

"I'd hate to have the job of cleaning this up," Phillips said. "Wonder where River Station is?"

"They just pulled in at the construction shack," Phillips said. "That must be the M.E. and lab, too."

They stood away from the rubble pile and watched the group of men approach across the bulldozed area.

"What took you so long?" Dunlevy asked as Lonto and Runnion walked up, followed by Victor Ruiz.

"Who's this, Lonto? Another member of the famed River Street Detective squad, known far and wide for screwing cases up?"

"Hello, Dunlevy," Lonto said. "This is Victor Ruiz from Miami. He joined us as observer today."

Dunlevy nodded. "Hope he's got a strong stomach," he said.

"So where's the body?" Runnion asked.

"You mean body parts," Phillips said. "Back of that pile there."

"You guys gonna need help on this one?" Dunlevy asked, suddenly serious. "It's nasty, so maybe we can help you out with some legwork."

"We'll probably need it," Lonto said. "Let's take a look."

80

The three new arrivals walked around the rubble pile from where Hooley and the lab men had disappeared. Both Lonto and Runnion pulled their handkerchiefs from their pockets as they looked at the limbless bodies. Victor Ruiz looked down calmly. There was a momentary flash of anger and pain in his eyes that passed quickly. He seemed unaffected by the smell. Hooley and lab men worked among the scattered body parts as though it was an everyday event. For the lab, it was an everyday event and dealing with the dead in any form was exactly what they did every working day. It was a thing they tuned out of their feelings and their thinking, or they would have found themselves another line of work.

Normally, at the scene of a homicide, the detectives would be jotting down such pertinent notes as where the body was found, time, cause of death, age, description of body to include height and weight, hair color, color of eyes. The trouble was, the body, or bodies in the rubble were decomposed; at least two of them were. The third, while probably no more than a week old, was missing legs, arms, and head. Lonto wrote only the time and place in his notebook and waited for Hooley to provide some information.

Looking at Ruiz, Lonto said, "Welcome to a new day at the office."

"These did not occur all at once," Ruiz said. "They used this place to dispose of the waste."

"A dumping ground for someone," Lonto said. "Must be a psycho."

"Or maybe one of these devil worship cults," Runnion said. "We had a bulletin on a cult in California that was sacrificing one person a month to some demon god or the other."

"I remember reading that," Lonto said. "Lots of crazies around."

Ruiz studied the bodies and shook his head. "I do not think so," he said. "I have seen this before in my country and Miami."

"You're talking about these Caribes again, huh?" Runnion asked.

"They cut off an enemy's head so he can't see them from the afterworld," Ruiz said.

"Superstition," Lonto said.

"Yes. But it is their way," Ruiz said. "Like once your people believed only a silver bullet would kill a werewolf. Or like we Catholics wear a cross to protect us from evil."

"This is Nineteen-eighty-six," Runnion said. "People don't believe in that crap now. Wearing a cross is just a symbol."

"Perhaps cutting off the head is also," Ruiz said. "To a Caribe it is the way, it has not changed."

"I thought you said these people had become civilized," Lonto said.

"I said they had adjusted to our ways, enough to live among us. They did not give up their old ways or customs."

"I don't think I'd like to be their enemy," Runnion said.

Ruiz smiled. "You are," he said. "In their language the word stranger means enemy. If you are not Caribe, you are an enemy."

"These could still be some psycho killings," Lonto said.

"There is a way to be sure," Ruiz said. "If the Caribe have done this, they will also take the heart."

He stepped into the rubble next to a body missing all its limbs.

"Are you finished?" he asked Hooley.

Hooley glanced at Lonto who nodded. "I've done all I can with that one," he said.

Without hesitation, Ruiz knelt and turned the body over on its back, then looked up at Lonto. "Caribe," he said coldly.

The chest cavity had been chopped cleanly open and both Lonto and Runnion were willing to believe the heart had been cut out.

"I suppose they cut the heart out to make them brave or

82

something," Runnion said. "What the hell have we got here, Tony?"

Ruiz shook his head and rose, brushing dust from his trousers. "They consider the heart a delicacy," he said.

"You mean a trophy?" Lonto said.

"I mean a delicacy," Ruiz said, smiling. "The name Caribe is our name for them and means cannibal. In your dictionary it means a tribe of cannibal people. As I told you they once lived throughout South America and the Caribbean. Now they are scattered. I believe some are here."

"Come on!" Runnion said. "Cannibals! They put that kind of crap on TV. That couldn't go on here without us knowing about it."

"How many missing person reports are filed each year in this city?" Ruiz asked. "How many people vanish that are not reported? There are enough I think."

"You're serious about this?" Runnion said.

"Let's hear him out," Lonto said. "There was a case in Wisconsin where three people disappeared and they found them in some guy's freezer, cut up like beef. He was eating them."

Ruiz pointed at the row of dark buildings. "Are they empty?" he asked.

"About six square blocks here have been empty for years," Lonto said. "What's on your mind?"

"Someplace near here they will have a meeting place," Ruiz said. "A place where the leader will speak to them and they share a meal that binds them together."

"Like one of these," Runnion said, nodding at the body.

"No, not always," Ruiz said. "They do not always eat man, it is a special ceremony for them now. But if they have to kill someone who is in the way of their business they will eat him if they can safely."

Lonto caught Hooley's attention and asked, "What do you make of this, Hooley?"

"Ask me that in about two hours," Hooley said. "Three

bodies for sure, we won't know until we get this rubble cleared. Some been here as long as six months. I never saw anything like this. From the looks of it, I'd say there could be others, hard to tell what's all here with missing limbs."

"Pat, see if you can get some extra patrolmen out here," Lonto said. "And ask Dunlevy to call in for some, too. We're going to need men to search this area."

"You got it," Runnion said, starting toward the car.

"All right, Ruiz. Where do you suggest we start?"

"There," Ruiz said, and pointed to a four-story apartment building near them. He was impressed by Lonto's willingness to accept the unusual. Part of his respect was due to the fact that they were both cops. But the major part of Ruiz's respect came from the fact that Lonto was a smart, tough, and persistent cop. That made him very dangerous to Ruiz.

"What are we looking for?" Lonto asked.

"A large hidden room where a fire would not be seen. In Miami they used an empty warehouse near a river and used the river to dispose of the remains of their victims."

"Why didn't you tell us everything about these Caribes before?" Lonto asked.

"Would you have believed me?" Ruiz asked. "In Miami we knew about the drugs but there was no proof of cannibalism, no bodies found, only traces of human blood at their meeting place. Those in charge chose not to report that because the publicity would be very bad for the city."

"You seem to know a lot about these people," Lonto observed.

"Yes," Ruiz said, "I understand them as did my father in our country." He stood looking at the deserted buildings for a long while before he went on. "It is difficult to find anyone here who believes such people exist."

"This doesn't happen every day, even around here," Lonto said. "But this sure as hell isn't a normal murder scene either."

Ruiz smiled. "To a Caribe this is normal," he said. "It is

not a wrong thing for them. A steer is butchered for beef. They even use a man's skin as leather."

Lonto shook his head. "Let's see if we can find this meeting place," he said.

They found the meeting place in what had once been 630 10 Avenue North, next to the building Ruiz had pointed out. In its time 630 had been a hotel, a Salvation Army Center, and finally a four-story flop house. Now, the rotting hulk was windowless, long abandoned even by the derelicts who sometimes slept in the condemned buildings along the block.

As they stepped into the large empty room that had been the lobby of the hotel, Ruiz stopped. "It is here," he said softly.

Lonto and Runnion looked around the empty, dusty room. They could see the men working on the rubble pile in the construction site through the broken windows.

"I don't see anything," Runnion said.

"The smell," Ruiz said, testing the air. "It smells like smoke and burned meat."

"You're giving me the willies," Runnion said.

Concentrating, Lonto sniffed. "Smells like smoke alright," he said. "Any chance these people might be around here?"

Ruiz shook his head and walked across the large room. In back of the long counter that had once served as the hotel desk was a door that opened on stairs leading down into a basement. The smell of smoke was stronger as they moved down to the dimly lit basement, their flashlights stabbing into the dark shadows along the walls. The basement was large and open, broken only by the trunks of concrete support pillars and the bright squares of small ground windows that were set into barred window wells along the outside of the building. The three men stood silently, trying to keep their breathing from sounding loud in the pressing silence.

Ruiz could feel the sweat pooling under his arms and leaking down his face as he fought the crowding fear in his mind. They are not here, he thought. They would not meet during the day.

A frantic, scrambling sound brought Lonto's light stabbing along the wall to pick up a rat who paused to glare at them with glowing red eyes. Lonto self-consciously pushed his half-drawn service revolver back into its holster.

"This way," Ruiz said, leading them toward the far wall.

Their steps echoed hollowly as they walked toward a dim circle of light that appeared to come from the floor above them in one corner of the basement. Under the hole, which had been broken through the floor above, was the remains of a fire that had been built on a broken slab of concrete. Around the fire the floor of the basement had been swept clean in a twenty-foot circle. On the support pillars at either side of the circle were tied the burned-out remains of torches. Outside the circle to one side was a pile of broken boards that had been used for the fire.

"Jesus fucking Christ," Runnion said. "I don't believe this."

Lonto turned and followed the beam of Runnion's flashlight where it played over a vague pile of white sticks in the corner. A large rat sat on the sticks and watched them.

"What?" Lonto asked. "The rat?"

"They are bones," Ruiz said quietly beside him.

Lonto stood silently for a long while, feeling an anger and revulsion he had not felt since his first year on the force. "Oh, my God," he said softly.

Detective Carl Pavolny and John Richards were sharing a bottle of whiskey and a line of coke at Richards's apartment while they went over the list of names and addresses of Eddy Loyd's customers that Pavolny had insisted all his pushers supply. A prudent move since pushers had a low long-term survival rate on the street, between getting hit by some street-wise rip-off artist or being arrested by some equally street-wise cop. In either case the pusher was out of business and Pavolny saw no reason for not having a customer list that would allow him to conduct business as usual. Pavolny and JR were sitting at a cluttered kitchen table. They were both sweating.

They had snorted a line of coke a half hour ago, before starting on the list, sorting the names and addresses to group them into areas.

"What it looks like to me, is he had about two hundred regular customers a week, some of them taking about an ounce of blow," JR said.

"Those are the ones who make the crack and sell it on the street," Pavolny said. "I know the prick was dealing on the street himself even after I told him not to be doing that nickel, dime shit."

"He had a good territory," JR said. "I know about half these guys myself. You figure Loyd's holed up with one of these?"

"He's got to be somewhere," Pavolny said. "I can't see where else he'd be. I'm sure the girl didn't know where he is."

"The word's out we'll give up an ounce of pure," JR said. "If any of the pushers know where he's at, they'd sell him in a second."

"Unless he's making them a better offer," Pavolny said. "I think the son of a bitch is trying to move in on our territory, maybe he's offering the pushers a better deal until he puts us out of business."

"Yeah, maybe, but where's he getting the stuff? You're the only one down here who's got the connections to supply in quantity." JR giggled loudly. "You and your cop friends made it too hot for any big supplier to operate down here."

"That's the advantage of being a narc," Pavolny said. "Just remember it was you and that bastard Loyd who gave us the names of suppliers to bust."

"You think he's going to snitch on us?"

"You can bet your ass he will if the cops get him first,"

Pavolny said. "He's got nothing to lose now. Not after leaving his fingerprints all over that knife he killed Joe with."

"He's a stupid bastard," JR said. "I can't figure him being able to take Joe the Dog down though."

"Joe got careless," Pavolny said. "Just make sure you don't."

"How the hell we gonna find that prick with all these names?"

"We start with the ounce dealers," Pavolny said. "We ask around and see if there's one around that isn't getting his stuff from us. Then we find out who is supplying him."

"Loyd maybe, huh?"

"He took plenty of my coke with him when he disappeared," Pavolny said. "I figure he'll move it."

"You want me to start looking up these ounce dealers?" JR asked.

"Yeah. I'm going to work on my snitches, see if there's a dealer out there we don't know about."

"This shit is bad for business."

"If we don't find Loyd, there won't be any business," Pavolny said.

In the park on Rice Street that evening, Victor Ruiz sat and watched the neighborhood families enjoy the fall colors and evening coolness. If you had lived most of your life in the lush greens of the jungle there is something stark and morbid about trees that seemed to die every year, to stand like picked bones against a dirty city background.

But it was a park, and most of those who kicked through the piles of fallen leaves did not know the ever growing greenness of a jungle, or the towering size of trees that reached hundreds of feet toward sunlight. There was a statue of a forgotten soldier at the edge of the park, reminding Ruiz of his father. When you needed a place outside to sit and think, even a park with leafless trees was better than sitting on a hotel fire escape.

Ruiz sat on a bench near the statue. Around him, he could

hear soft conversations in Spanish and the sound of kids playing. In an hour he knew the park would be deserted as the families sought refuge in their apartments and the city's human predators waited in the park for a late worker or someone foolish enough to cross the park after dark. In his country the people stayed out of the parks out of fear of the police as much as of the criminals. In these cold, American cities the people did not fear the police so much, but seemed to dislike them except when there was trouble. No matter, a policeman did not need to be liked—only respected.

He listened to the growl of the city in the background, and wondered if his fear would ever leave him. It was the smell of smoke and meat that brought the fear, he thought. The old fear from when he was a boy and they had killed his father, sharing him among the clan while he lay tied in a hut at the edge of the meeting place. When the soldiers and police came they had killed many Caribes that night, but he would always remember the smell that was there.

He had sworn on his father's grave that the Caribes would pay. He would hunt them no matter where they went until the clan was broken and scattered. He knew their leader was here, he told himself. The one who held them together and kept the old ways alive. If the leader died without passing on the knowledge they kept so secret there would be nothing to hold them together. They would be easier to hunt and punish then.

Coming to this precinct may have been a mistake. Was it? he asked himself. The ones I want are here. But he was too much of a cop not to understand that Lonto had a deadly thorough patience when he investigated. He could not ignore the danger a patient, honest cop was to him.

He would need to mislead these police when he could, and he would avoid killing any of them if he could. It was only that they did not understand the logic and need to deal with the Caribe at their own level. It was not a crime to exterminate vermin. It would be a great crime not to hunt them, to ignore they were here someplace. There was an emptiness inside him along with the fear.

It was a matter of honor, the way he had chosen, and the choice had condemned him to turn away from a life he had wanted for himself. Since the first one, he had known that there was no way to cross back into a system of laws that would not allow him the personal satisfaction of revenge that had driven him from his own country to a country whose laws seemed written to protect the animals he hunted. A place where they could hide and be protected except from someone who knew them.

Ruiz left the park, walking slowly toward the lights along Rice Street, thinking that perhaps tonight he would find one who would lead him to the leader.

6

They had called Lietutenant Jaworski from the construction site and advised him of the situation. Being experienced cops they were well aware of what a hot shot reporter could do with a story that just might be the city's first case of cannibalism. The lieutenant had sworn steadily into the telephone and then said, "I want a lid put on this, and I want every man on the squad in here at shift change," and then he asked if they were sure. They told him they were more sure than they wanted to be. He swore again and hung up. When they got to the squad room, they filled him in more completely on the grisly details, and Jaworski decided it was time to pass the buck on up the ladder to call the police commissioner and let *him* decide how tight the lid would be kept on this one.

The police commissioner, who was looking forward to an after-work drink with his secretary, glanced at his watch and informed Jaworski that it was damn near quitting time, and couldn't this wait until morning.

Jaworski cleared his throat and said, "Well, some bunch of nuts down here is killing people for their barbecue and I figured you might like to know about it."

The police commissioner was silent a moment, then said, "Did I just hear you right? What's this about a barbecue?"

Jaworski patiently explained exactly what he was talking about, taking a perverted pleasure in describing the situation right down to the clean pile of bones found in the deserted building that Hooley had identified as human.

The police commissioner had never heard of a more revolting situation in his life. Why, these maniacs must be absolutely insane to think that they could do this in his city and get away with it. Jaworski agreed that the situation was insane by any standards. Nonetheless, from the available evidence, the crimes were committed over a six-month period and the criminals, insane or not, had gotten away with it up to this point.

The situation was unthinkable, the police commissioner decided. True, his years on the police force had been spent behind a desk uptown after a brief tour in one of the more affluent suburbs, but he was certainly aware of the occasional heinous crime that happened in the city. What he couldn't understand is why this Lieutenant Jaworski was bothering him with the gory details of a crime committed by some bunch of lunatics. Why didn't they get busy and arrest these lunatics?

"Well," Jaworski said, "we are certainly going to do our best, sir. I would really *like* to get busy on this case and make some quick arrests, but there is a very good chance that the newspapers and TV stations will not see this as an average event. In fact, I think that if news of this gets out we are going to be up to our ass in reporters down here. And I just happen to think you might want to have some advance warning."

"I see what you mean," the police commissioner said. "How many people know about this?"

"Just my homicide detectives know the whole story," Jaworski said.

"Keep it that way," the police commissioner said. "No leaks, you understand? I'll get back to you after I've apprised the mayor of the problem." He hung up.

The mayor was not pleased with the news. In fact he was furious, and wanted to know what kind of a goddamn police force they had in this city when people were being killed, and eaten, for Christ sake, on the goddamn streets during an election year? What the hell was going on in this city anyway?

"Well, sir," the police commissioner started, but the mayor broke in saying, "While you're at it, maybe you can tell me why there's been two, possibly three, unsolved homicides in that part of the city during this past week, and now this mess, when my aide informs me that your last quarterly report indicates that that precinct has a sufficient number of men to police it. Maybe you can tell me what the hell is going on down there," the mayor shouted into the phone.

"Well, sir, my budget," the police commissioner started, but the mayor went on. "Or maybe you can tell why an adequate police force hasn't been established down there after we earmarked funds for an increase of manpower in our high-crime areas?"

"We had a new precinct station built," the police commissioner defended.

"Police protection doesn't mean a new goddamn station house!" the mayor shouted. "Police protection means having enough trained officers on the streets to get the job done and keep this kind of thing from happening. Do you understand that?"

"Yes, sir, I," the police commissioner began, as the mayor went on, "Now I want some results on this and I want this cannibal crap kept so quiet that it makes Reagan's first arms sale look like national news. Do you want this city splashed all over every news service in the country in an election year?"

The police commissioner certainly didn't want the city in the news in an election year, especially since a mayor was the one who appointed police commissioners, so he said, "Yes, sir, I'll get right on it, top priority."

"You had better get some results," the mayor said, and hung up.

The police commissioner did not like it when an attempt

to pass the buck resulted in the problems ending up right back in his lap. But, as he was a firm believer in the old saying that shit runs downhill in a chain of command, he immediately dialed the River Station's number and asked to talk to Lieutenant Jaworski.

Lieutenant Jaworski had all the problems he needed that evening, what with a crooked cop on the squad, a handful of murders, the regular run-of-the-mill robbery, assault, and rape cases. Jaworski was not a big fan of the police commissioner to begin with, the commissioner being a man who was absolutely sure he knew everything there was to know about police work, based, of course, on his vast experience—one year as a patrolman, one arrest on an assault charge that was later thrown out of court. The police commissioner did not have a great deal of love for Lieutenant Jaworski either, because Jaworski was the sort of old hard-line asshole who said exactly what he thought, letting everyone in the area know his personal opinion of a police commissioner who had less real field experience than a six-month rookie on the Strip.

"What are you doing about this mess, Jaworski?" the commissioner asked.

"Following procedures," Jaworski said. "We're doing a room-by-room search of all the deserted buildings and questioning anyone who worked or lived near the area."

"And?"

"We placed the building under twenty-four hour surveillance as of four this afternoon and doubled the patrol cars in that area. Not much else we can do until we get some lab reports and know what we've got to work with. Do we have a lid put on this?"

"Of course we have, damn it," the commissioner said. "All the news service gets is we're investigating a murder. What about this Ruiz?"

"He seems to be an expert on this bunch. Worked on a case like it in Miami."

"Then use him," the commissioner said. "How many men have you got on this?"

"Two. Lonto and Runnion. The Highland Park Station has offered some help with the legwork."

"Put some more men on it," the police commissioner said.

"Sure. Who are you sending me?"

"Put some more of your own men on it."

"I can't spare any men, sir. As I said in my last report we're undermanned and overloaded. Besides, right now any more than the team that's on it would just be in the way. That's the way I'm going to keep it, sir."

"This is your hot potato, Jaworski," the commissioner said. "You understand what I'm saying, Jaworski?"

"Yeah," Jaworski said. "I know it's my ass."

"You bet it is," the commissioner said, and hung up.

"That didn't sound like an invitation to dinner," O'Malley said.

"Might even have been an ass chewing," Lonto said, grinning.

The squad was seated, or leaning against the wall in Jaworski's office, trying to keep from smiling. An ass chewing is always interesting when it's not your ass that's being chewed.

"The commissioner says no news leaks, not a whisper about cannibals or anything else. What we have is an unidentified homicide victim. Clear?" Jaworski asked.

They all nodded.

"I want some action on this," Jaworski said. "Where the hell is Ruiz?"

"Went back to his hotel," Lonto said. "He gave us a good rundown."

"Okay, then," Jaworski said. "One more thing. Uptown has been running a phone tap on a pusher up there.

"They say there's going to be a drug drop to a mailbox at Thirteen-twelve Cedar Avenue around three tomorrow afternoon. The building's deserted and there's no cover in the area for more than a one-man surveillance. The dope's going to be picked up around six tomorrow afternoon." Jaworski looked at his watch. "That's about twenty-five hours from now. Uptown wants one of us to get there about five and get a picture of who picks up the junk."

"No arrest?" Runnion asked.

"Just a picture," Jaworski said, looking around the room. "Looks like you're it, Lonto. You're the only one who's used a long-range lens before. You stay, the rest of you get out of here."

"What if this guy picks up the junk early?" Runnion asked.

"He won't," the Lieutenant stated, "this guy's very careful they said. He'll be there on time and not before or later."

Lonto stood by the window and waited as the rest of the squad moved out of the office, then he turned to the lieutenant and asked, "Since when did I have any experience with a telephoto lens? I can't take a clear picture with a Polaroid for Christ sake."

"I know that," Jaworski said. "Tommorow, I want you to be free and over there by three-thirty. I'll meet you."

Lonto was silent for a long while.

"This is a set-up then?" he asked.

"The whole squad knows the dope will be there from three to six, and no one should be on stake-out until five. Let's see if one of them decides to pick up the dope early."

"I don't like this, Lieutenant."

"Goddamnit! Do you think I like trying to set up one of our own?" Jaworski shouted. "Would you like it better if I turn this over to those headhunters on internal security?"

Lonto was silent.

"Let's clean up our own department, Lonto," Jaworski said. "At least we can do that. Are you in or out? I won't order you to do that."

"Where do we meet?" Lonto asked.

"I'll let you know," Jaworski said, tiredly. "Go on, get out of here and try to get some rest." Before Lonto reached the door, he added, "And try to get us some results on this Caribe thing." He shook his head. "Jesus, what a city this is."

Runnion was waiting for him in the squad room and they

walked in silence downstairs to sign out and then to the car. The evening traffic was heavy as they neared Davis Drive. With the car window open, the cool evening air was thick with exhaust fumes as Lonto edged the vehicle into heavy traffic. He glanced sidelong at Runnion, who was staring straight ahead, and then asked, "Going to see Lin or work tonight?"

"Both if I can drive out there and get back by eight," Runnion said. "What did Jaworski want?"

"Just some crap about that drug drop tomorrow."

"Why the hell doesn't uptown handle that?" Runnion wanted to know.

Lonto grinned. "They can't spare the men," he said. "Besides they figure it's our precinct."

"How do they figure we got time?" Runnion asked. "You supposed to just drop everything else."

Lonto shrugged. "I can spare an hour," he said. "I'll get there at five and leave at six-fifteen. If he's not there by then, they can take their own pictures."

"We get all the shit details down here."

Lonto was silent. He didn't like lying to a man he'd risk his life with, a man who was a friend. He didn't like the idea that he couldn't trust him and maybe didn't really know Runnion.

"Any word on Lin's operation?" Lonto asked.

"She's next on the list they tell me," Runnion said. "Sometimes I feel like hell because I find myself wanting some stranger to die whose kidney will be compatible."

"I think I'd feel the same way if Robin was waiting for a donor," Lonto said. "Traffic's heavy tonight."

"What really burns my ass is some rich foreigner can come to this country and get a donated organ," Runnion said. "Money talks in this country. Money will buy you a damn kidney when our own people have been waiting months for one."

"I thought there was a national waiting list," Lonto said.

"There's supposed to be, but if you come up with the money you'll see how fast they can find you a kidney."

Lonto was silent for several moments. He took a deep breath, and said, "Pat, this morning Robin said you had finally got a loan. Lin told her, something about the police retirement fund."

"Guess she misunderstood," Runnion said, looking away.

Lonto said nothing. He watched the traffic through the windshield ahead, and then blew the horn at a car trying to change lanes ahead of them.

"You did manage to get a loan though, right?" Lonto asked.

"Yeah, I got one," Runnion said, suddenly antagonistic. "What the hell is this, Tony. I'm your partner. We're not married you know."

"Okay," Lonto said. "Forget it."

"Anything wrong with taking out a loan?" Runnion wanted to know. "I'm working two jobs you know."

"Forget I asked," Lonto said. "You want me to drop you at Vernon Avenue?"

"Yeah," Runnion said. He looked at Lonto suspiciously, silent until they parted on Vernon Avenue.

At nine-thirty that night John Richards threw back the dirty gray sheets on his bed and rose to prepare for the night's business. His first act was to snort the two lines of coke he had prepared on the dresser next to the bed. Then he pulled the curtain back to stare out the window at the dark city streets.

At nine-thirty it seemed as though the city would pause for a moment to change its beat from the hurried buzz of the day workers leaving the streets after some shopping to the more upbeat tempo and flashing neon lights of a city coming alive for a night life filled with drunken laughter and crowded bars and those city dwellers who used the cover of darkness to stalk the streets for a victim.

It seemed the city had two faces. During the day, it wore

the face of a growing industrial city, busy with the task of work and the daily wage. At night, it put on its bright lights, and spread its doors wide to tempt the citizens to get down and party.

Those citizens who did not leave the city after work knew all about the bitch city after dark, locked their doors once they were home from work, and remained inside until morning.

JR stood by the window watching as the rush of the cocaine built in his body. He swore silently, and reminded himself that he would have to ask Pavolny for more cocaine tomorrow, so that he wouldn't be running out. With Eddy Loyd and Joe the Dog out of business, he was steadily finding new customers. He had promised to keep everyone supplied who had the price.

The street outside was fairly crowded for so early and he thought about walking down to the corner bar for a few quick ones, but he had promised himself he wouldn't be out on the streets at night unless Pavolny was with him. Not until they got that bastard Loyd anyway.

He turned away from the window and prepared for the evening's business, counting out the packages of cocaine he kept in the top drawer of the dresser. The small, one-gram envelopes sold for seventy dollars a package. The larger packages were for the street dealers who paid thirteen hundred an ounce as long as they bought four ounces a week. On the bottom of the drawer was a .45 automatic which he checked and shoved under his belt. You couldn't be too careful when you were dealing with some of these hop heads.

The man watching John Richards's apartment waited across the street in the shadows. His fingers caressed the handle of the knife inside his jacket. Wearing dark clothing, he knew he blended into the blackness of the doorway he stood in, but he remained absolutely still as he had for the past hour. Only his eyes moved to search the street, his senses tuned to the sounds and feel of the night. He knew this would be the night. After this, there would only be the cop to kill.

He remained in the shadows, watching as John Richards's customers began to arrive. It was a little after twelve when he crossed the street and entered the building. The hall was empty when he reached the apartment door and knocked three times, his hand gripping the knife tightly.

He could hear footsteps approaching. Quick steps of a man who was impatient and wanted to get the night's business over with.

"Yeah, what do you want?"

"Candy, man, what else?"

He heard the safety chain rattle and watched the doorknob turn until the lock clicked before he threw all of his weight against the door sending it smashing back into Richards.

Then he was inside swinging the heavy knife as Richards pulled the .45 from his belt. The long blade buried itself in Richards's neck before he could aim the .45, and sent the gun clattering across the floor as Richards stumbled back. He swung the knife again and again. Richards stayed on his feet, holding his bloody arms up to ward off the slashing blade.

"You stinking bastard," Richards said.

The man swung the knife again, beating down Richards's arms and feeling the hollow thump as the long blade chopped solidly into his skull. Richards stiffened, and then fell forward, his face colliding wetly with the floor.

The man swung the knife again, swearing at Richards, then stood over him. He watched the body twitch until it was finally still.

The man wiped the long blade on the back of Richards's shirt before he began to search the apartment.

Homicide, if it doesn't personally affect a man, is a fairly average event for a cop. Nonetheless, cops tend to take all homicides as a personal affront because it is the taking of a man's life, and every cop, every day, is faced with the chance that his own life might be stolen from him. A cop really can get involved in the investigation of a homicide case and more than anything would like to devote all his working hours to any homicide on his caseload.

Unfortunately, there are other crimes to deal with in the everyday life of a precinct. And at the River Station precinct there are a good number of crimes such as robbery, rape, burglaries, muggings, assaults in various degrees, car thefts, gang wars, prostitution, and the usual domestic disputes, all of which take a great deal of time out of a cop's working day. Most of these crimes are assigned to the robbery, burglary, vice, or other squads at River Station but if a homicide detective answers a call that turns out to be a burglary, he is responsible for the initial investigation and report, which is sent to the squad handling that particular crime; and all those investigations and reports can keep a man busy when he could be working on his own case.

It's not so easy to find time for your own case when you are scheduled for night court, either. For cops, night court is a waste of valuable time since it was created to handle what are considered petty crimes, to unburden the courts during the day to handle the more serious crimes, which may involve months of jury trials and appeals. No one likes night court detail, especially when they have a murder case to work on.

Neil O'Malley and Pete Mills were scheduled for night court. They were especially displeased on this particular evening because the most serious crime on the charge sheets was a breaking and entering, which meant they would spend their evening escorting minor lawbreakers over to the courthouse where a tired judge would either release them with a fine or sentence them to serve between thirty and ninety days in the county jail.

Since Mills lived in the suburb of Apple Grove, and after five years had not learned how long it would take him to drive to work, he arrived at the station his usual five minutes late thereby missing the first round of fun and games for the evening that consisted of escorting six prostitutes from the holding cell into the waiting police van parked outside. The "girls" had not had a great deal of good things to say to O'Malley during the procedure.

As Mills strolled up, he waved happily at the girls in the van and winked at O'Malley.

"Traffic was a bitch coming in," he said.

"You say that every time you're late, and you're late every damn night," O'Malley said. "Just once I'd like to see you get in here the usual fifteen minutes before shift starts."

"I love it when you're in a good mood," Mills said. "That way I know I have a full eight hours of enjoyment ahead of me. We got time for a cup of coffee?"

"You think I'd be standing out here waiting for you if we had time to screw around. These cases come up in fifteen minutes."

"Let them wait. Five minutes before the judge and they'll be back on the street selling it by ten o'clock." He grinned at the hooker giving him the finger through the van window. "This is no time for romance, honey," he said. Then to O'Malley he asked, "So how many new bodies turned up today?"

"Three or more," O'Malley said. "It's hard to tell because parts of them were used as the main course of a cookout. If you'd get here on time you'd know all about it."

"I'm in love," Mills defended. "I've only been married seven months. I got better things to do than hurry off to work."

"You were never on time before you were married."

"Who got the case anyway?" Mills asked.

"Lonto and Runnion," O'Malley said. "This past week has been a bitch for homicides. What the hell is going on out there?"

"This is the armpit of the city," Mills said. "Anything can happen down here."

"It's the asshole of the city."

"But I wouldn't work anywhere else," Mills said.

"Yeah," O'Malley said. "Let's get the ladies over to court, maybe we'll have some time later to work on the Galeas case."

Lieutenant Isaac Frienberg did not have anything to distract his attention from his work. As senior medical examiner at the police lab Isaac could justifiably delegate all incoming cases and fieldwork to his assistants and simply review their findings and doing so would allow him to go home each night at a respectable hour to his family in South Hampton.

Forensic medicine fascinated Isaac, especially when the case being investigated was a challenge, or had occurred in unusual circumstances. There was nothing at all usual about a case that involved cannibalism. In fact, Isaac could not remember ever hearing about a case that involved cannibalism. There was no question in his mind that this was an authentic case, much as he would have liked it to turn out as a hoax, like the time the guys at River Station had sent him a shrunken monkey head and requested an identification on the man. But how much question can there be when you have three dismembered bodies, all with limbs and other body parts missing, and you also have a box of bones, which have been gnawed clean not by rats but by persons unknown. After examination of the bones Isaac was absolutely sure that more than one person had been involved.

It did not take a mental giant to determine this. Since the human teeth and mouth structure are unique among mammals, teeth leave very distinctive marks on any item that is chewed on.

The teeth marks on the bones were clearly human. There were, of course, several bones which also carried the twin chisel marks of a rat's teeth. That was to be expected in a city where rat bites were common on any corpse that had been in an alley for more than a few hours. Hell, rats commonly bit people who slept in an alley and sometimes they bit children left unattended in their beds. The marks of rat teeth you could expect; marks from human teeth were unusual. He could, if the case was ever brought to court, prove that evidence of cannibalism was clearly present. Given a suspect's dental chart or an impression of his teeth, he was sure he could match the teeth marks on the bones to a particular person.

He was also sure, from the preliminary tests, that the bones found inside the building had come from the three bodies next door in the morgue. He was feeling particularly fascinated this evening because he was absolutely sure this case would make him a nationally recognized expert on cannibals since he was pretty certain he would be the *only* forensic expert in the county who had ever worked on such a case. He should make copies of all his findings to send to other police labs. He would send them if they ever decided to let this case go public.

Identifying the remains of the three bodies in the morgue wouldn't be as easy as it might sound. Identification could be accomplished in several ways. Often he would supply Missing Persons with photos and a description and wait for a relative or friend to come down to make an identification. Another way was to identify a person through matching dental charts. And there was always the old dependable fingerprints—if they could be taken, they could be matched by a computer in a matter of minutes if they were on file.

Unfortunately, none of these basic three methods would work in this case. They would not work for some very good reasons: the bodies did not come with heads, hands, or legs. Therefore, looks, dental charts, and fingerprints were out of the question.

What Isaac did have in the morgue was enough to determine sex, age, height, weight, body structure, race, hair color, and an estimated time of death. That would be forwarded to Missing Persons who might be able to match the descriptions to someone in their files.

Isaac did not expect the three bodies to be positively identified, but he was willing to turn his full attention to attempts to gain some additional information for investigating detectives.

7

José Lopez learned early in his life to distrust all strangers. Distrust is an excellent character trait for a dope pusher to have. His father, on the other hand, had not been distrustful enough and had ended up very, very dead, a process which had taken a long half hour while José had watched. He had learned his lesson in a shanty-town ghetto before his mother had brought the family north to a city ghetto where the lesson applied equally well. As a growing boy, he had watched his cousins bash in the skulls of a good number of strangers, who had been stupid enough to wander into their territory. When you were dumb as a goat you deserved to be treated as a stupid goat, José figured.

José had been considered a man by his family at fifteen. Now, at twenty-one, he was a respected leader, but their family was smaller. José still disliked and distrusted all strangers but he knew that to stay ahead in the world of cocaine pushing you sometimes had to deal with strangers who had been recommended by other strangers who bought your dope.

Now, he sat in the rear booth of a small café named The Gold Cup and knew that he was being watched by the tall Hispanic outside, long before he entered the café. The man was pretty much as his contact had described him, right down to the gold earring in his ear. He was wearing jeans and a black T-shirt under a Levi jacket and had checked the place out for fifteen minutes before he had decided to come into the café. He walked directly to José's table, approaching with the sure, quick stride of a cat. He looked down at José and said, "You look more like a cop than the man I want."

"And you look like a narc in drag," José answered.

"How do I know you're not wired?"

"Same way I know you're not," José said. "Why don't you sit down so everyone can go back to drinking their coffee?"

"Yeah, what the hell," the man said. He slid into the booth across from José, and then placed his elbows on the table. "So you're the man, huh?"

"Maybe yes, maybe no," José said. "Let's hear what's on your mind."

"I thought Martinez filled you in."

"I want to hear it from you," José said. "Start with a name."

"Name isn't important," the man said, smiling. "I'm from Colombia. You ever been down there?"

"We're talking about you."

"Okay, I've been in the states about two years doing a little business with a guy called Joe Wells. About a week ago he gets himself killed and I wind up with no connection. Now I got some very good customers waiting uptown and nothing to sell them."

"I never heard of this Joe Wells."

"They called him Joe the Dog on the street."

"What was he giving you?"

"I usually need a half pound a week. Right now I need a half kilo to catch up."

"What were you paying?"

"A grand an ounce, pure, because I step on it once before I sell."

"It ain't much."

"It's more than these pushers down here are buying," the man said. "I can use a kilo or more a week by next month."

José was silent for a few moments. He kept watching the man intently. Then he broke the eye contact and said, "So you want a half a kilo now, huh?"

"That's right."

"You got the money on you?"

"Do I look stupid? I got the money but I want an intro to your supplier too."

"Not a chance," José said. "You deal with me."

"I deal with the supplier," the man said. "I can give him more business from uptown than you can from a dozen pushers down here."

"You're loco," José said.

"You deal with these small-bag crack dealers like Martinez down here. Uptown, I deal with ounce customers. You turn me on to your supplier and I can get you some of that uptown action too."

José studied him in silence again. He leaned back in the booth and took a cigarillo from his pocket. He lit it slowly, blew out a stream of strong smoke, and said, "There is no way my supplier will deal with a stranger."

"So introduce us and I won't be a stranger."

"Not a chance."

"Why don't you ask him? See what he says, or I go shopping someplace else."

"Like where?"

"Joe Wells must have had a supplier."

"So why ain't you looking for him then?"

"Don't play cute with me, José. You know and I know it ain't healthy to do business with a supplier who starts getting his pushers knocked off. I don't want to get into any drug war, I just want to do some business. If I have to I can go to Miami to shop."

"I can't turn you on to my supplier," José said, "not now anyway."

"Why not?"

"That isn't the way it works."

"Yeah. How does it work?"

"Here's the deal, take it or leave it. I supply your stuff for a few deals. If everything is business and we don't have any problems, then I see if the supplier will deal direct with you and you cut me in one some of the action uptown. I don't know if you're solid, you know."

"Okay. We deal together for a few weeks, but you tell your man I want to meet soon."

"I decide when you get to meet anyone," José said.

"Okay, okay," the man agreed, and leaned back in the booth. "You got a sample of the blow on you?"

"Now, you must think I'm stupid," José said, shaking his head.

"Where then? It has to be tonight."

"Place called Dusty's on Rice Street," José said.

"I don't do business in any bar."

"You got a car?"

"Sure."

"We'll make the deal in your car in front of Dusty's Bar then."

"What time?"

"How long do you need?"

"I'll be there in an hour, that okay?"

"I'll be there," José said.

Dusty's Bar was a dive as rank as the worst along Rice and River Street. Ruiz knew such bars well, a place where the whiskey was watered, the bar girls well past their prime selling years, and the hookers working the drinkers were either fast, hard, and cheap or young, inexperienced, and also cheap; in either case anyone in the market for a quickie stood a fifty-fifty chance of catching a dose of something to take home to the little lady. The sidewalks in front of the bar were almost empty and littered with garbage. A drunk was sleeping in the doorway of the pawn shop and a young, dark-haired girl in shorts and a red blouse that were too thin for the evening's coolness was working the sparse evening traffic from under the streetlight fifty feet away. The flashing lights from the bar sign cast red light into Ruiz's car as he pulled into the curb and parked in front.

He sat silently in the car, waiting and watching the young

girl under the streetlight as she offered a view of her legs to the occasional passing car and slumped back against the lamp post disinterested when they passed.

He wondered what he was doing in this ugly city so far from home. He imagined himself back home, walking along the river with his father only to discover a group of Caribes waiting along the path. Even his father, who had killed many of them for the bounty the government paid, had not been fast enough to protect the two of them from their sudden rush.

Even now he woke up screaming at the thought.

In the darkness down the block, Ruiz could see José Lopez as he stepped out of a doorway and walked toward the car. He looked through the window into the back seat before he opened the door and slid onto the front seat.

"Alright," José said, "let's see the money."

"Where's the blow?" Ruiz asked.

"Right here." José opened his jacket and laid four packages of white powder on the seat between them. "The money?" he said again.

"Try the glove compartment," Ruiz said.

Jose turned and opened the glove compartment. As he reached for it he caught a motion out of the corner of his eye and turned to see Ruiz aiming a small automatic at his face. The muzzle seemed very large at this range.

"Just freeze right there, José," Ruiz said, smiling. "If you move even a little I'll kill you right here."

He reached gingerly toward José, patted him down, and pulled the .38 special from a belt holster.

"You're not going to need this," he said, smiling, "now where's the knife?"

José was silent.

Ruiz shoved the muzzle of the automatic hard against José's neck, forcing his head back against the window as he continued to pat him down, finally finding a long-bladed knife in a leg sheath and slipping it into his own pocket.

"Now sit back against the door with your hands flat against your knees."

"You don't think you can get away with this, do you?" José asked.

"Of course I will," Ruiz said.

"You better start running far and fast," José said. "We sure as hell will find you."

"You won't find anyone."

"What do you mean?"

"I don't worry about dead men," Ruiz said.

"You won't kill me in your own car. Right on the street?"

"It's not my car," Ruiz said. "I stole it about a half hour ago."

"What makes you think I would make a delivery alone?"

"That won't make any difference at all to you."

"If I'm not alive my people will know who ripped them off, won't they? Where does that leave you? You pull that trigger and they'll find you. They'll hunt you down no matter where you go."

"That's what I'm counting on," Ruiz said. "I want them to come to me."

"You're crazy," José said, sweating. "You don't know who you're dealing with here."

"Yes, I do," Ruiz said, and shot him.

The body lay like a bundle of rags in the gutter in front of the now dark bar.

The street was empty of pedestrians, leaving only the police moving in the white glare of lights set up by the lab unit. A patrol car was angled in against the curb on each side of the body, their top lights blinking a red message along the street and sending any late passersby detouring around the block. The night medical examiner and an assistant knelt beside the body.

On the sidewalk the two patrolmen who'd first responded to the call were talking to the man who reported the body after leaving the bar. The man's name was Leroy Snyder.

He kept looking at the body and saying, "He just opened the door and pushed the body out, then he smiled at me. I ain't never been so scared in my fuckin' life."

O'Malley and Mills arrived at the scene at one thirty-two. They had completed their escort duties to night court at midnight, and had managed a brief stop for dinner at The Bull Pen near the station when the call came in. O'Malley looked down at the shattered face and the single bullet hole just above the bridge of the nose without expression. Mills joined him, saying, "You notice something familiar about this one?"

"Yeah," O'Malley said. "Besides being dead he's got an ear missing. What the hell is going on down here? We got some sort of gang war going?"

He looked at the two patrolmen on the sidewalk, "Come here a minute. You took the call didn't you?"

The older of the two patrolmen walked around the body and stood beside them.

"Who reported it?" Mills asked.

"That guy there, name's Leroy Snyder. Came out of the bar in time to see the body pushed out of the car."

"He get a look at who did it?"

"Says he did. Trouble is he's got half a load on and I don't know how much he really saw."

"But he actually saw the body dumped, huh?"

"Hell, ask him. He's the most cooperative witness I've ever ran across."

They walked Leroy Snyder over to their car and introduced themselves. Leroy was wearing a heavy navy-blue sweater and a blue stocking cap. His corduroy trousers were tucked into rubber boots that reached up just below his knees. He grinned at the two detectives, enjoying all the attention he was getting.

"What time did you come out of the bar, Mr. Snyder?" Mills asked.

"Like I said, I got off work about ten-thirty. I work at the slaughterhouse, you know, cold as hell in there so I stop for a few shots before I go home. It was about twelve-fifteen when I come out the door there."

"Did you look at your watch?" O'Malley asked.

"What for?" Leroy wanted to know. "I looked at the bar clock before I left. I always leave at twelve-fifteen."

"You work this late every night?"

"Six nights a week."

"What kind of work do you do?"

"I work as a cutter in the cold room. I also stop for a couple to warm up before I go home."

"Where do you live?"

"Sixty-seventh Street in Walkers Bluff."

"And you seen the body being dumped when you came out of the bar, is that right?" O'Malley said.

"I was already out of the bar when he dumped it."

"What do you mean?" Mills asked.

"I was standing on the sidewalk lighting a cigarette when the door opens and he pushes the body out. I almost shit my pants."

"There was just one man in the car?" O'Malley asked.

"That's all I saw."

"Did you see him clearly?"

"The bar sign was on then," Leroy said. "I seen him real clear. He smiled at me, then closed the door and took off."

"Describe the man," Mills said.

"He was a spic, not that I got anything against them. I even work with some; niggers, too. Some of them are alright," Leroy said.

"How tall would you say he was?"

"He was sittin' in the car. How would I know?" Leroy said. "He was maybe thirty-five, forty, black hair, even had a little mustache."

"Would you recognize him if you seen him again?" O'Malley asked.

"I ain't lookin' to see him again," Leroy said. "Any man who pushes a stiff out in front of me and smiles ain't no one

I ever want to see again. That's one hard-ass spic, let me tell you."

"You recognize the dead man?" Mills asked.

"No."

"What kind of car was it?"

"Looked like a blue Pontiac Fiero, Eighty-five I think, might have been black. Hard to tell in the bar lights. My brother-in-law had one like it."

Mills was writing in his notebook.

"Did you get a look at the license number?"

"I didn't look at nothing but him," Leroy said. "He just closed the door and drove off."

"Anyone else on the street?" Mills asked.

"He drove past some hooker standing there by the streetlight but she got the hell out of here fast."

"What did she look like?" O'Malley asked.

Leroy shrugged.

"Okay, give us your full address and phone number and you can go home. We'll be in touch with you later."

"What for?"

"Well, for one thing we'll want you to look at some mug shots. You're the only one who can identify this guy," Mills said.

"Just remember that I sleep mornings," Leroy said. "I ain't got time to be screwing around a police station."

"We'll try to make it convenient for you," Mills said. "Thanks for your help."

"Let's talk to the M.E.," O'Malley said.

The rest of the morning was routine.

They waited for the medical examiner and the police photographers to finish before they went through the dead man's pockets. They found a wallet, car keys, an empty pistol holster attached to his belt and an empty knife case on his ankle. They also found a package of cocaine under his body when they moved him. The wallet contained six hundred and twenty-two dollars in fifties, twenties, and singles.

There were no identification cards or driver's license in the wallet, nor were there any pictures, social security card, or alien identification card, which the detectives thought was strange considering their own paper-packed wallets. The ambulance had carried the body off to the morgue when they found the empty .380 shell case on the pavement. It had been run over by a car.

It was just at shift change that morning when they got back to the squad room.

In the madhouse of the squad room at shift change, Lonto laid the three murder case files on his desk and tried to find a connection between them. The first, the probable murder that had taken place in Eddy Loyd's apartment was an unknown; no victim was connected there as yet. The second, the mutilation murder of Joe Wells was definitely connected to Eddy Loyd—his fingerprints were on the murder weapon—but Ruiz had suggested that the method of killing was like the Caribe killings. And finally, the bodies that were found at the demolition site were definitely tied into the Caribe group, but was Eddy Loyd tied into them also? The one thread that tied all the murders together was cocaine, but cocaine was a part of a lot of crimes in the city. Ruiz had said the Caribe group considered all strangers as their enemy. So how would Eddy Loyd be connected? Unless he was not a part of the group and only pushing for them. The simplest way to deal with the cases would be by investigating the cases involving Loyd as one case, and the Caribe murders as another, though they weren't sure at this point if the Caribes existed. Cannibals yes, but who was doing it was unknown.

After ten minutes of reading, Lonto finally gave up and closed the files, knowing that the bodies found at the construction site were likely to remain unidentified, and unless they got some breaks the case would go unsolved. It was not a cheerful thought. After all, how would you like to know cannibals are roaming the city and the cops can't catch them?

"What do you make of this, Tony?" O'Malley asked, setting the partly smashed .380 cartridge on his desk.

"Another three-eighty, huh?" Lonto said, holding it up. "This from the homicide last night?"

"Yeah, same m.o. as the Galeas case. One shot through the head and an ear cut off."

"Which ear?" Lonto asked.

"Right side, both times," O'Malley said. "Lab says they make these cartridges in Brazil."

"So?"

"Why would anyone risk bringing a gun and ammo into this country? You can buy a pistol in damn near half the bars around here."

Lonto studied the cartridge. "Maybe there's something special about it."

"Yeah. Well, if you get a chance today ask the lab to see if they can check it out more, will you? I'm heading home."

Lonto watched him leave, and studied the cartridge for several minutes more before he checked his address book, picked up the phone, and dialed a number.

Herman Schultz was a gunsmith who had once helped the police identify a rifle used in a sniper case. He was a man in his sixties, with gray hair and square, wire-rimmed glasses that he always wore low on the bridge of his nose while he peered at his customers over their tops. During the past thirty years Schultz had become known as the best gunsmith in the city, at least as far as the police officers were concerned. He would not only find an officer the best service revolver available and tailor the trigger pull to fit that officer's preference, but would shape the revolver's grip to fit his hand. To Schultz a revolver was a personalized tool which must fit the man whose life might depend on it. For the police, his charge for personalizing a revolver was only what the material cost, which made him very popular with the underpaid cops. Schultz also knew more about firearms and ammunition than any man Lonto had ever known.

When Lonto called him that morning, he was patiently

carving a hunting scene on the walnut stock of a deer hunting rifle. The phone rang several times before he set his tools down and picked it up.

"Herman Schultz here," he said.

"Hello, Mr. Schultz," Lonto said. "I don't know if you remember me, this is Detective Tony Lonto at the River Station. You helped us with a sniper case a few years ago."

"The Swiss mountain carbine that was used with a one-hundred fifty-gram silvertip load. And you had your revolver trigger pull adjusted. How's the revolver now?"

"Fine," Lonto said. "It doesn't pull to the left now."

"Good," Schultz said.

"I've got an unusual cartridge here that I hope you can give me some information on. It's a three-eighty pistol cartridge and our lab says is made in Brazil."

"What are the markings on the base?" Herman asked.

"It has three-eighty and PBX seven," Lonto said, reading.

"Mm," Schultz said.

"I'm wondering if any standard three-eighty ammo wouldn't fit this weapon just as well? Why would someone bother to bring the shells into the country?"

"Cartridges to fit the three-eighty can be bought in most gun shops," Schultz said. "However, the PBX seven three-eighty is a special cartridge developed for the police in South America. Not all the police I understand, but what they call 'special' police. The PBX seven fits their automatic pistols and a small machine gun like the Israeli."

"Anything special about the cartridge itself?" Lonto asked.

"Most three-eighty's come with a copper jacket bullet," Schultz said. "The one you have there is made with a flat nose wad cutter, or dumdum, and is loaded with more powder for greater killing power. It is also made with a soft nose slug and a shape slug that will penetrate most bulletproof vests."

"Sounds like it's made special to kill men," Lonto said.

116

"That's why it was developed," Schultz said. "I understand it's effective."

"Sounds like it should be illegal," Lonto decided.

"It is illegal," Schultz said. "In fact they are not sold anywhere, certainly not in this country. The PBX seven is made only for the special police. Where did you get the cartridge?"

"Here in the city at a murder scene," Lonto said. "I don't suppose you know which countries supply their police with them, do you?"

"That's easy," Schultz said, "it's listed right here. Brazil, Argentina, Colombia, and Peru. It's been manufactured for about twelve years now."

"Could be a lot of them around by now," Lonto said.

"Yours is the only one I've heard of," Schultz said. "I'm sorry I couldn't be more help."

"No, you did great, Mr. Schultz. You gave us a lot more than we had."

"Anytime," Schultz said, and hung up.

The problem was, as Lonto saw it, that Schultz had given him a lot more information than he had expected. It had also given him the type of information that led to more questions. Couldn't Schultz have just said "It's a cartridge made in Brazil" and left it at that? It would have been a snap then to toss the cartridge back to O'Malley and tell him the lab was right. Now, he was faced with the chance that since Victor Ruiz, Detective Victor Ruiz, who was formally of the Colombia police, and the Miami police, could have once been a member of the "special police" Schultz had mentioned. After all, the .380 murders hadn't begun until after Ruiz had arrived, and a man doesn't need to be hit between the eyes with a possible lead to justify looking into it further. Maybe he should just turn the information over to O'Malley and let him worry about it. But since Ruiz was a visiting officer, you had to be very damn careful about looking into his past record and the fewer people who knew about it the better it would be. Nonetheless, he intended to find out if there was any connection between Ruiz and the homicides, and the place to start was in Lieutenant Jaworski's office.

Jaworski was used to the unexpected in his line of work and especially when dealing with Detective Lonto, who would at times run his cases on intuition, which more times than not solved cases. He had what Jaworski called a "feel" for a case that most good cops developed. Jaworski respected Lonto's gut feelings.

"What the hell to you mean, you want a look at Detective Ruiz's file?" Jaworski asked. "You can't look at a man's personal file just because you're nosy, let alone look at a man's file who's just on temporary duty here."

"Is there a file on Ruiz?" Lonto wanted to know.

"Not here at this station," Jaworski said. "I'm sure they have one downtown. But the police commissioner would have to approve for you to look at that."

"Can you find out if there is a file?" Lonto asked.

"I suppose I can. Captain Daniels would know," Jaworski said. "This is a very long shot you know."

"I don't want to marry the man or check his credit rating, Lieutenant," Lonto said. "I just want to find out if he was in a special police unit in Colombia. He must have submitted a resumé to get on the force in Miami."

"I'll ask Daniels if there's a file, and if there is I'll see what he can get out of it," Jaworski said. "Now get out of here."

As Lonto turned away Jaworski asked, "What are you working on today?"

"Catching up on reports," Lonto said. "We don't have anything from the lab on the cannibal case so it's Eddy Loyd and paper work until Pat gets back."

"Get me some action on those three bodies," Jaworski said, and turned back to the papers piled on his desk.

The Missing Persons Division was located in the basement of the building which also housed the police lab and the city morgue, on the corner of 27 Street and Bryant in

South Hampton. The city jail and district court shared the building with the county attorney. At one time or another, every detective in the city found that he, or she, was spending more time out of his work week at the district court building than they were on the street, either in court, at the district attorney's office, viewing a line-up, or at the police lab, so Pat Runnion was familiar with the procedures when he arrived. Pinning his police identification card to the front of his zipper jacket he made his way downstairs and introduced himself to the gray-haired patrolman at the desk.

The patrolman's name was Harry Bullock. He had twenty-eight years in the force and was waiting out his retirement in two years. He had a bad heart and a stiff leg and wondered at times if his life had been wasted.

"You guys must think we got nothing to do down here but worry about an occasional kid who just might have been reported missing," Bullock said. "Let me tell you, we got stiffs and unidentified bodies that go back ten, fifteen years. We probably got two, three hundred records on missing kids just this year alone."

"This one would have been reported missing in the last few weeks," Runnion said.

"In that case there are probably only fifteen or twenty," Bullock said. "But that's just from the city. We probably got two hundred maybes from around the country."

"Maybes?" Runnion asked.

"Missing kid inquiries from out of state," Bullock said. "The ones that say the kid may be in our fine city. Is your kid a local?"

"We have no idea," Runnion said.

"You guys are a lot of help."

"I suppose I'll have to look at all of them."

"The trouble with you guys," Bullock said, "is that you don't have any idea how much work goes into keeping these files straight and orderly so that once in a while we're able to identify someone. You guys come in here and screw up the files so bad that it takes me a week to put them in order again."

"Well, I'll make sure all your files get put back where they came from," Runnion said. "Believe it or not, we actually use a filing system at the River Station, too."

"Another thing you guys like to do is remove things from the files," Bullock said. "They take forms out of one file and put them in another file because they think that will make things more interesting for us guys here."

"I'll make sure everything goes back in the right file," Runnion said, "that is, if I ever get to look at any of them."

"Patience," Bullock said. "You guys are always in a hurry to screw up the files."

"I'm in a hurry to get started at least," Runnion said.

"How far back do you want to go?" Bullock asked.

"Better make it a couple of months."

"I thought this kid's only been missing a few weeks?"

"She might have been reported missing before that."

"Alright," Bullock said, "come in here and look. We got them filed alphabetically and broken down male and female, both in city and out of state and by month."

"Thanks," Runnion said.

"Latest files are on the right there," Bullock said, pointing. "If you need any help, yell."

Runnion sighed, looked at the large green filing cabinets. He carried a wooden chair over to the cabinets on the right and began to search the files labeled: FEMALE, AGES 10 TO 18 INCLUSIVE.

The work was, as is most policework, routine. What he hoped to find was a missing persons file on a black-haired girl between the ages of twelve and eighteen, on the theory that if there was such a report, it might lead them to a missing girl who just might have been murdered in Eddy Loyd's apartment. The lab report had fingerprints and body hair found in Loyd's apartment and it was now their job to identify a person to match them, like finding the old needle in the haystack. But when you're investigating a murder, you work with what leads you have, no matter how slim they are. The problem with the slow grind of the daily routine is that it gives a man too much time to think. And when you're looking at report after report, each one telling a brief story of a person's life, you get bored with who has a tatoo where or an interesting birthmark in such a location and you begin to consider such things as the problems in your own life.

Problems that have you smoking two packs of cigarettes a day and a feeling of desperation inside that you can't share with anyone. Everyone in the department knew what the problem was with Runnion's wife. He knew that they had covered for him at times when he was late for work because he was too tired from working two jobs to get up in time. He also knew that Lonto was concerned about him because Lonto was his best friend as well as his partner.

There were not many cops around that would be as good a partner and friend as Lonto. Would that friendship still be there by the time this was over? There was a lot of strain between them at present. Pat felt he couldn't completely trust Lonto anymore, and he knew he was avoiding the talks they used to have. There wasn't time for that now, there was only time to think about Lin's operation and the money he needed for that. He hoped Lin never found out what he did to get the money. Lying to her about the loan had been a mistake but he had forgotten that Lin and Robin shared the events of their lives like schoolgirls. He just couldn't let her find out or she'd blame herself. She didn't understand that he didn't care what happened to his future as long as she got well. He wondered if Lonto would lie to Robin to keep her from knowing something that would hurt her.

His attention returned to the file he was reading. The missing girl's name was Alice Foster. She was sixteen years old when her mother had reported her missing ten days ago. Her physical description was, height: 5' 3"; weight: 115; build: slim; hair: black (exceptionally long); eyes: hazel. The girl had never been fingerprinted, and there were no tattoos or birthmarks on her body. There was a photo of a slim, pretty girl in the file.

The girl was still missing. Runnion saw that her home address was in the Tandy Ridge suburb of the city and wrote the address down in his book. He wondered if this could be the girl who had been in Eddy Loyd's apartment.

On a warm, clear, fall morning you would think that the citizens around River Station would mellow out and enjoy the seventy degree temperature before winter got a dirty-Marvin crotchhold on the city and everyone began to freeze their ass off every day. But in the last half hour the squad room had gotten very busy.

It must be a full moon, Lonto decided. There was something about a full moon that brought the nuts out like shoplifters at a Christmas sale. The cops at River Station rarely enjoyed what could be called a slow season, but it appeared that things were starting earlier than usual this morning.

The man handcuffed to the chair beside Detective Washington's desk had a broken nose and was dripping blood steadily on the floor.

"What the hell happened?" Lonto asked Washington quietly.

"He resisted arrest," Washington said. "What'd you want me to do? Pat him on the back?"

"A hundred and twenty pound kid resisted arrest so you broke his nose?" Lonto asked softly. "The judge is going to take one look at him and cut him loose if he doesn't charge you with assault on top of it."

"Fuck him," Washington said. "He's just a pusher."

"He tried to shake me down," the man said.

"Shut up, asshole," Washington said. "What the hell's the matter with you, Lonto?"

"He broke my nose 'cause I didn't have any dope."

"I told you to shut up."

"I'll tell you what's the matter," Lonto said, "if Jaworski walks in here you're going to be up on department charges."

"He's a *pusher* for Christ sake!"

"I don't care if he's an ax killer," Lonto said. "Take him down to medical and get him fixed up."

"Alright, alright," Washington said. "I didn't know cops were such bleeding hearts down here."

In the detention cage across the room, two middle-aged drunks in business suits and wearing black-and-white convention hats were pressed against the security screen watching the action. "Let us out of here," one said, "we ain't done a damn thing."

"The patrolman says you propositioned three women at a bus stop," Lonto said. "As soon as one of them signs a complaint we're going to book you."

"What the hell, we didn't mean any harm," the drunk said.

A hooker, seated beside Detective Gonzalez's desk, looked at the two drunks in the cage and called, "How about it honey, how much you pay for some of this?" She cupped her breasts at them. "I'll take you both on at once."

"Who's your girlfriend, Gonzalez?" Lonto asked.

"Guy said she took his wallet at a motel," Gonzalez said. "They were scrapping on the street."

"I didn't take any wallet," the girl said, "the cheapskate didn't want to pay me."

"How much for the both of us, honey!" one of the drunks shouted.

The girl smiled brightly at the drunks. She was a good-looking woman in her mid-twenties with a strong slender body, firm breasts, and short black hair. She was wearing a short blue skirt and a white blouse. "I'll take you both around the world for a hundred bucks, make you both happy."

Turning to Gonzalez she said, "How about letting me go, okay? We could have a good time later. You're a good lookin' hunk, you know."

"Man said he wanted to make a complaint," Gonzalez said.

"So where is that creep?" the girl asked. "You make him pay me my fifty bucks, huh?"

"Where's the guy at?" Lonto asked, grinning.

"Said he'd drive right over," Gonzalez said, "should have been here by now."

"Let's see your tits, honey," one of the drunks called.

"What you see is what you get," the girl said, pulling her shoulders back to make her breasts push against the thin blouse. She smiled at Gonzalez. "Come on, let me go," she said, "That cheapskate is back in his office by now."

Gonzalez shook his head. He had other things to do besides waste his time booking a hooker who wouldn't be in jail more than two hours. Most of the squad ignored the working girls, but the man had insisted. Looking at the girl with appraising eyes he began to think that it wouldn't be a bad idea to let her walk and take her up on her offer later. She *was* a good-looking woman indeed. She winked at him and crossed her long legs with deliberate slowness, allowing a brief glimpse of her black panties.

"What do you think, Tony?" Gonzalez asked.

"It's your bust," Lonto said. "I'd say the john is back at his office by now. She didn't have his wallet, did she?"

"He didn't pay me either," the girl said. "That's what we were arguing about."

"We'll pay you, honey," one of the drunks called. "Room Six-ten at the Parkview Hotel."

"Bring a girlfriend," the second drunk said.

"I got everything you need," the girl said. "I'll screw your socks off."

The drunks cheered. They were having better luck in jail than they had at the convention. Gonzalez was considering letting the girl go when a patrolman pushed open the door and waved at Lonto.

"May as well cut them two loose," the patrolman said. "The ladies decided not to sign a complaint."

The drunks began to applaud.

"What about me?" the hooker asked.

"Yeah. What about her?" one of the drunks asked.

"Oh, what the hell," Gonzalez said, tearing up the report he'd been writing. "I don't have time for this crap." He winked at the girl. "Next time get your money first."

"Take them two downstairs too, will you, Vince?" Lonto asked, as the phone on his desk rang. He picked up the receiver.

"Homicide Squad. Lonto," he said.

"This is Detective Roman, Fourth Ward. We had a homicide last night over on Forest Avenue, after midnight the medical examiner says. Guy by the name of John Richards got himself cut all to hell. Name mean anything to you?"

"Not a thing," Lonto said, watching Gonzalez escort the hooker and the two drunks from the room. It looked like a family reunion.

"Thing is," Roman said, "it looks like this killing may be tied into a case you're working on."

Lonto picked up a pencil. "Go ahead," he said.

"The lab called a few minutes ago," Roman said. "Guy named Hooley is the medical examiner on the case, seems to know what he's doing. A couple of bloody prints at the murder scene belong to a guy named Eddy Loyd. You working a case that he's a suspect in, too?"

"He's a suspect in one, maybe two homicides."

"Well, he's a sure suspect in this one," Roman said. "His prints are all over the apartment."

"How was this guy Richards killed?"

"The M.E. said he was killed with a heavy-bladed knife; guy looked like he'd been worked over with a meat cleaver."

"Uh-huh," Lonto said.

"Same guy. Same m.o., right?"

"Sounds like it."

"What I want to know is how should we work it?" Roman said. "You want me to start on this or do you want to handle it?"

"Cedar is way the hell out of our precinct," Lonto said. "I know it is. Look, I'm not trying to dump this case on you, I just don't want us covering the same ground when we don't need to."

"We haven't been able to put a lot together on the case yet," Lonto said. "One thing I'm pretty sure of is that Loyd's not in any of his usual holes. He may be laying low over in your area. I'll send you copies of our reports on the case so far."

"That will give me something to start on," Roman said.

"Our victim here was a coke dealer," Lonto said.

"This one, too. Maybe we have some sort of drug war here," Roman said.

"Loyd's a pretty big dealer," Lonto said. "If you come up with anything, let me know."

"Okay," Roman said. "Send a patrolman with the files."

"They'll be there this morning," Lonto said.

8

The newsstand on the corner of Fourth and Silver was closed when Lonto and Runnion arrived at eleven-thirty that morning. They found Trash Can O'Toole in a booth at the coffee shop across the street. He was not having a late breakfast, but using the phone booth in the coffee shop to lay off some of the morning's bets he'd taken on the day's races.

He sat opposite Lonto and Runnion and listened to what they wanted. Then he said, "Sure, I remember Princess. She was a real good-looking girl. Last I heard about her she moved uptown."

"You know what her name is?"

"Lois something or other," Trash Can said. "Memory ain't as good as it used to be nowadays. What'd she do?"

"We just want to ask her some questions."

"She was a pretty nice kid," Trash Can said. "Didn't get into dope or stealing from her customers. I hear she's doing real good uptown."

"Can you locate her for us?"

"Princess will be easy to find," Trash Can said. "She ain't trying to hide from anyone I know of."

"How about Eddy Loyd, anything on him yet?" Lonto asked.

"*He's* the one hiding from everyone," Trash Can said. "I tell you, Tony, that's one hard man to locate. No one's seen him. There's not even any rumors about where he might be; like he's vanished completely."

"With a murder one charge hanging on him, it figures," Lonto said. "Well, get back to us on Princess as soon as you can."

Detective Carl Pavolny had been nervous ever since he had checked in to work and had learned that John Richards was now in the morgue and whoever had murdered him had cleaned his room of any drugs or money there might have been. Pavolny knew exactly how much cocaine or money should have been in Richards's apartment last night. Between Joe the Dog and Richards, Pavolny figured he had lost a little over fifty thousand dollars worth of coke, plus the twenty thousand he had lost when Eddy Loyd had double-crossed him. That was seventy grand that came out of his pocket because his supplier in Miami didn't do any credit business. Worse yet, without his ounce dealers to move the stuff to the street pushers, he was out of business unless he could line up some more dealers.

Business was not on his mind that morning. With Eddy Loyd out there and his two dealers dead it was time to get out of the cocaine business for a while. He had made that decision when he realized that he was being followed last night. He had spotted the same Hispanic on his tail three times last night and being a cop it didn't take him long to figure who Eddy Loyd had teamed up with to put him out of business. Well, he wasn't going to get into a territory war with a bunch of spics from that part of the city called Little Havana, he didn't need that kind of heavy action.

What he was going to do was take sixty days of the vacation time he had saved up and spend it fishing down in the Keys. He would take the money he had in his two safety deposit boxes and the cocaine that remained and tuck it away down there. And after his vacation was over, and Eddy Loyd figured everything was going his way he would come back and Eddy would start getting a lot of pressure from the narcotics squad, or maybe Eddy would make a mistake and get himself arrested. Either way, Eddy Loyd was going to end up on a slab in the morgue. One thing that stupid fuck hadn't realized was that he had the whole police force to back him up. No matter what Loyd did, he couldn't win, because the narcotics squad could make life very tough. Pavolny intended to make it so hard for Loyd's people to operate that they would realize that Loyd had to go, and once that happened his own people would feed him to the cops and Pavolny would be waiting. After that, it wouldn't be any problem to start his own business once more.

All he had to do was be careful and take care of himself until his vacation began tomorrow afternoon. He wondered where that spic bastard was who had been following him.

Lonto and Lieutenant Jaworski sat in an apartment on the first floor directly across from 1312 Cedar Avenue, with a pair of binoculars and a camera. They had arrived with a telephoto lens at the boarded up and deserted building at three-forty that afternoon, getting into the empty front apartment late after finding the door had been locked and having to return to the car for a crowbar to break the lock. Through a two inch space between the boards nailed over the window they had a clear view into the doorless entryway across the street and the mailboxes on the right.

It was a very clever drop arrangement for the dealers who used it. The buildings on both sides of the street were empty and deserted, there was no traffic, or any reason for a car to be parked anywhere on the street, thereby restricting any observer to the building and offering a hard-working drug dealer a much better chance of escape.

Since neither Lonto or Jaworski was interested in making a street arrest that fall afternoon, they were not concerned that it would take a sledgehammer to break out the boarded front entrance before they could reach the street. They would, as Jaworski had said, be content to take some pictures of whomever picked up the dope.

There was only one problem.

They had arrived within a half hour of the scheduled drug

drop. It was now three minutes after six and not only had there not been a pickup by a crooked cop, it was beginning to look like the dealer was not going to show to make a pickup either.

Watching the building with the binoculars, while Jaworski waited silently beside him with the camera, Lonto thought more about his fellow cops than he did about any dealer showing up. His thoughts in particular were on Runnion because after lunch he had decided to question Windy Sterling once more since Lonto was scheduled to return to the station house. Lonto did not like remembering that Windy Sterling's apartment was only six blocks north on Cedar, because he knew they had agreed that the woman was not going to give them any leads about the business partners of the deceased Joe Wells. Nor did he enjoy thinking that there might be another reason why Runnion wanted to remain in the Cedar Avenue area earlier. He dreaded the thought that one of his fellow officers would show up at the drug drop, and yet he knew that a stake-out for a crooked cop was small potatoes considering the cases they were working that week. But a crooked cop on the squad was so damn personal, even knowing that once he was caught the squad would regroup into teams and he would be back to the daily grind. The damn thing about it, he didn't want to be faced with the adjustment needed to work with a new partner.

"Anything out there yet?" Jaworski asked, lighting a cigar beside him.

"Nothing yet. The only things I've seen on that street was a cat and that van that went through."

"It's damn near six-thirty," Jaworski said, "we'll give it until seven. After that uptown can get their own pictures."

"How good was this information on the drop anyway?" Lonto asked.

"It was solid. They have an undercover cop and a phone tap working on this one." Jaworski was silent a moment. "At noon they said the drop would be made on schedule."

"Well, if it's there, no one seems interested," Lonto said. "Wait a minute, we've got a bite maybe, car coming down the street."

Jaworski picked up the camera and peered through the boards. "Looks like one man," he said.

The car pulled into the curb directly across from the two detectives. The angle of their position above the street prevented either man from seeing the driver's face and when he left the car, their only view of him was from the back. The man hurried up the steps into the entryway and Lonto sighed with relief when the man turned and began inspecting the mailboxes.

"He's a stranger to me," Lonto said, hearing the clicking of the camera beside him as Jaworski took the pictures.

"Keep on him," Jaworski said, "see if he makes the pickup."

Across the street, the man opened the second mailbox from the far end and seemed to pause for a moment before he hurriedly began to open the other boxes.

"Looks like a man who forgot his box number," Lonto said, watching the man frantically searching.

Jaworski snapped a picture. "What time did we get here?" he asked.

"About twenty to four," Lonto said.

"The drop was at three," Jaworski said, "someone got here before we did."

"Someone sure got here before that guy did," Lonto said, watching.

"Only our squad knew the damn timing," Jaworski said, swearing as he continued to take pictures while the man came out of the building and drove off.

"We just let someone get away with a couple of ounces of coke," Lonto said. "All uptown gets is pictures of some guy searching mailboxes."

"Yeah," Jaworski said, "I should have timed it better."

Lonto wondered why Jaworski didn't sound too worried about the screwup.

She sat in the window seat and watched the evening traffic in front of their apartment. It was after seven, but she reminded herself that she had decided she would not call the station every time he was late in coming home from work. According to the day shift schedule, he should be on duty from seven-thirty until three-thirty. Of course, that schedule had no basis in a cop's real daily shift schedule that was posted each month only for the benefit of record keeping, and did not really apply to the hours a cop worked. The hours a cop worked depended on the type of case he happened to be working on. For instance, if he was working on a burglary, mugging, or some everyday drug case, he could be expected to come home and enjoy a meal at a reasonable time. On the other hand, if the cop was working a homicide case, then there was no time that you could expect him home. Homicide cases were a twenty-four-hour job and unfortunately Tony was a homicide detective. He had promised to come home early tonight, and she had made the roast he always liked, now getting dry in the oven.

Not that he would complain. He always seemed content just to be home and to talk. She must remember to talk to him about her finding a job. It would help her stay busy until there would be a baby. She smiled at the thought.

She turned to look at the clock, wondering if she shouldn't call the station and ask just this one time. Maybe the roast wouldn't be too dry if she turned the oven off and covered it now.

Turning back to the window she watched a car turn onto the block and smiled at the sight of a crooked right headlight. Tonight, at least, he was only a little late. She quickly left the window seat and closed the curtains so he would not know she had been worried.

The city received a sample of what the next few months would bring that night. At eight o'clock in the morning the temperature reached the day's high of 64 degrees. At the River Station, the new heating system decided it was not time to begin the winter's work and refused to turn on. Everyone in the squad room worked in his overcoat and fondly remembered the cool heating system at the old station house that kept the station heated despite the numerous problems. Being the first real cold snap of the season, the detectives repeatedly stated that winter was going to be a bitch this year and remembered past winters when a sudden blizzard would transform the city into a lifeless polar tundra.

Lieutenant Jaworski's office was as cold as any in the building. He was not, in fact, feeling cold at the moment. When he first arrived at the office he had gotten a call from the uptown narcotics squad regarding the drug drop last evening, followed by a call from the police commissioner's assistant informing him that the police commissioner expected a progress report on the cannibal murders at ten o'clock.

The present call was from a reporter on the city's weekly scandal sheet. He asked to speak to whomever was in charge of the homicide squad and was promptly transferred to Jaworski's office.

"This is Lieutenant Jaworski," he was told.

"Lieutenant," the reporter said. "This is Noah Powers of the *City News*. I wanted to check out a possible story."

Jaworski's first impulse was to hang up the phone. River Station's past experience with the *City News* had been complete publicity disasters for the River Station cops, making them feel like idiots who were assigned to this section of the city because they were unqualified to work anywhere else.

"Yes, Mr. Powers," Jaworski said, "what can I do for you?"

"We got a tip last night . . ."

"Who gave you this hot tip?"

"The caller was anonymous," Powers said.

"So, what was this hot tip about?"

"The man suggested that we contact you regarding some bodies found in Old Town a few days ago. Some of the bodies had parts missing, is that correct?"

Jaworski was silent.

"Lieutenant Jaworski, is that information true?"

"I wasn't at the scene," Jaworski said. "I suggest that you contact the Police Commissioner's office and ask for the information officer."

"Would they have information on the case?"

"Why don't you ask him?"

"Who are the investigating officers on this case?"

"The names of our officers are not supplied to anyone who calls in here," Jaworski said. "The information officer will give you any news on the case that's available."

"Would you personally have any information. . . ?"

"I'm up to my ass in information down here," Jaworski said. "We have file cabinets overflowing with information on assaults, rapes, burglaries, bum burnings, robberies, homicides, car thefts, every crime in the book we have information on. But, from your past experience with us, I'm sure you remember that we are public servants paid to protect the public and not to serve as an information center for reporters. The public information officer is paid to provide information so I suggest you call him. He should be delighted to hear from you."

"Come on, Lieutenant," Powers said, "give me a break."

"Look, mister. I don't intend to give out any information on an ongoing investigation."

"I'm just trying to earn a living."

"So are we," Jaworski said. "Your paper makes it harder."

"Is Detective Lonto still at River Station?"

"He doesn't like you and your newspaper any more than I do," Jaworski said.

"I'd like to talk to him."

"He's busy."

"When will he be free?"

"Christmas would be a good time to call."

"I just want to know if there's anything to this tip on parts of bodies being missing."

"Call the commissioner, Powers," Jaworski said. "They have all the information available."

"I'm going to find out what's going on," Powers said.

"Good luck," Jaworski said, and hung up.

Then he sat and thought about it. The situation was not good. If the newspapers were already nosing around, it wouldn't be too long before there was a leak on the case and it was front-page news. Jaworski sighed and picked up the phone to call the police commissioner and report there was no progress on the case.

The call from Trash Can O'Toole came at nine-thirty that morning. The desk sergeant took the call, and transferred it to Lonto's phone.

"River Station," he said. "Detective Lonto."

"Hi, Tony. It's Trash Can."

"Morning, Trash Can, what've you got for me?"

"Princess's real name is Lois Denton. Wasn't too hard to find her."

"Where's she at?"

"This is just questions, right Tony? She ain't in any trouble?"

"Like I said, we just want to talk to her."

"Because she's got a nice thing going and don't want any trouble."

"Where's she at?" Lonto asked.

"You know the Chilton Arms downtown?"

"You're kidding!"

"Her and a girlfriend's got a suite on the seventh floor, number seven-sixteen."

"If she can afford a place there she must have a good thing going," Lonto said. "Any idea what it is?"

"She's still turning tricks, Tony. Only now instead of fifty-dollar johns she gets five hundred for a night. Guess the guys are usually from the Foreign Trade Building. Anyway they can afford her."

"Will there be any problem getting to see her?"

"Naw, she left word at the desk to send you up," Trash Can said. "She'll be in all morning."

"Thanks, Trash Can," Lonto said, and hung up. Turning to Runnion, he said, "We found Princess."

The Chilton Arms was a prestigious hotel near the hub of the uptown business district. The hub of the city had been constructed to provide visitors at the Foreign Trade Center and convention halls with everything from shopping malls to an amusement park and outdoor markets within a six block area. During working hours, the city hub had a population density equal to a business district in Hong Kong. It was the big business part of the city where the shops were expensive and the rent high. And where you could find money being spent, you could find the girls practicing the world's oldest profession. On Silver Street the girls worked the bars, massage parlors, or in one of the several cathouses along the street. On Rice Street the girls worked wherever an interested customer might happen by, including the sidewalks and parks. The owners of the massage parlors and cathouses advertised them under such names as Sally's Sauna, Bambi's Hot Baths, The Professional Touch, or An Afternoon Affair, but whatever the name, you paid your money and took your chances. When the more violent crime rate dropped, or the street hookers began straying into the housing areas away from the red-light district, the cops raided several of the cathouses and made street arrests to send a message, but the raids were usually conducted by the vice squad. Some of the River Station cops were regular visitors at a massage parlor of their choice on a business basis on the theory that if a café would give a hard-working cop a free cup of coffee then a massage parlor should provide a free sample also. It was considered a working arrangement and preferable to paying a bribe.

As you moved further uptown, were the city council insisted they had an image to protect, the girls became more creative in their advertising, though some still worked the plush bars in low-cut evening gowns. Uptown, the low-key advertisement suggested an intimate evening with a young lady from the Star Modeling Agency or the World Escort Service. The owners of these highly profitable businesses also had a working arrangement with the cops, which kept most freelance competition out of the area in return for keeping their girls healthy and reasonably honest, as long as the well-heeled clients were happy. The girls were something of a necessity to the happy completion of the megabucks business deals.

Lonto, perhaps, was a tolerant cop. Or an honest one, depending on how you looked at it. Growing up in the Walkers Bluff district above Silver Street he had accepted early in life that the working girls on the street were a normal part of city life. But he had never visited one of the massage parlors on the free cup of coffee theory.

Lonto and Runnion were not interested in the legal aspect of prostitution or the working arrangement the girls might have with the uptown cops. They were only interested in the name Princess might provide them with. At the hotel desk, Lonto said, "Lois Denton's apartment, she's expecting us."

"Your name, please."

Lonto held his badge and identification card in front of the clerk's face. "Detectives Lonto and Runnion."

The man nodded. "You're expected," he said, "take that elevator there. It's suite seven-sixteen."

Lois Denton was wearing a black silk robe that clung suggestively to her slim body. Petite with long straight black hair and large brown eyes, she wore a single gold chain around her neck and large gold hoops in her earlobes. She greeted the detectives with a smile that seemed completely real.

"Good morning," she said. "Isn't it beautiful for this time of year?"

"I'm afraid it won't last," Lonto said, "but it's been a nice Indian summer."

"Come in," she said, leading the way into the living room. She walked with the practiced sway of a woman who enjoys being watched, her tight little behind jiggling actively in the tight silk, her black hair hanging loose down to her shoulders.

"Can I offer you a drink?" she asked.

"We're on duty," Lonto said. "I'm Lonto, this is Runnion."

"I know," she said. "Sean told me about you."

"Who?"

"You know. Trash Can, he's a sweet old guy."

"So that's his name," Lonto said, grinning. "I don't think he ever told me."

"He told me lots of things about you," she said. "He even pointed you out to me once when I was working down there."

"Miss Denton . . ."

"Lois," she corrected.

"Lois, we won't bother you long. What we need is the name of the cop who's been supplying cocaine on River Street."

"Boy, you guys don't fuck around do you?" Lois said, surprised. "You want information that can get a girl killed."

"If you believed that you wouldn't have told Windy Sterling about him," Lonto said. "We just want to get our information straight."

"I don't like to get mixed up with cops," she said. "He might have friends down here. Then where will I be?"

"Look, Lois, when we take this guy off the street there won't be any way he can connect you to the bust."

"I don't know that much about him anyway," she said. "He just came around for his free lay, you know how it is."

"How about the cocaine?" Lonto asked. "How do you know about that?"

"He made a deal at my place once before I moved," Lois said, "told me to take a walk but I went to my girlfriend's next door. The walls are like paper in that place."

"Did you actually see him with cocaine?"

"Oh, sure. Once he was feeling really up and offered me a hit. He had a lunch pail full of one-ounce packages."

"When was this?"

"It must have been six, seven, months ago," she said. "I kept away from him as much as I could. The girls were all scared of him. He beat Bonnie up so bad she was in the hospital for three months."

"You don't have to be afraid of him, Lois," Lonto said, "your name will never come up."

"Bullshit," Lois said.

"What?"

"The day cops start protecting hookers from other cops my mother will get in this business."

"We want this guy off the street," Lonto said. "If Trash Can told you anything about me, he's told you I take care of my sources. Your name won't be brought up under any condition."

"How about the strong silent one here?" Lois asked, watching Runnion.

"He's my partner," Lonto said. "Ask Trash Can."

"I already did," she said. "He thinks I should help you."

"Well?"

"Okay, okay," she said. "What the hell, the creep's name is Pavolny, Carl Pavolny. I read his identification card once. He's a narc from Fourth Ward."

"Jesus Christ," Runnion said.

"Can you describe this man?" Lonto said.

"Big, ugly man, fat," Lois said. "I don't think he ever takes a shower."

"Would you identify a picture of him?" Lonto asked.

"I'll never forget that creep," she said. "Would you guys like some coffee maybe?"

"I think I need some," Runnion said.

The squad room at River Station had not warmed up much by noon. It had, if it was possible, gotten colder, which did nothing to brighten the grim mood of the detectives who moved around in hushed silence still wearing their overcoats and talking in subdued tones to each other. There were two major reasons for the grim atmosphere; first, the presence of a representative from the police commissioner's office and an agent from the State Bureau of Criminal Investigation who were presently closeted in Jaworski's office, and second, cops don't like it when a cop goes bad.

There was little doubt now that Pavolny had gone over the line in a way that made every cop feel dirty and somewhat guilty. The girl had positively identified Pavolny, and a rapid check by the B.C.I. agent had turned up the fact that Pavolny had closed out his savings accounts in two banks as well as emptied his two safety deposit boxes that morning. Further checking had added the information that Pavolny had taken a sudden two-month leave of absence and had booked a flight to the Keys leaving at six o'clock that evening. They were now waiting for a search warrant to insure that Pavolny did not make his flight.

Detective Isaac Frienberg called Lonto at twelve-thirty and was greeted by an impatient sounding voice.

"River Station, Lonto here."

"Tony, this is Isaac at the lab. What's going on down there? It sounds like our morgue. Did you guys go on strike or something?"

"We're not having a great day down here," Lonto said. "No heat in the building for one thing."

"And?"

"A visit by some unhappy brass," Lonto sighed. "Believe me, you don't want to know about it."

"You're right, I don't."

"So what have you got to cheer up my day?"

"Well, it's purely an educated guess, mind you, but I may be able to bring some brightness into your world."

"I'm all ears," Lonto said.

"About this cannibal case," Frienberg said. "I'll send you a full report later, right down to what was eaten and when. But for now we've been putting most of our attention on getting some identification on the bodies."

"Identification would give us a starting point," Lonto said. "Right now we have nothing to go on."

"That's what we considered was most important anyway."

"Did you get an identification on the bodies?"

"Without fingerprints we have to rely on other identifying features, several of them in fact."

"How many were you able to get from these bodies?"

"None of the standard ones. You have to agree that with only a body trunk there isn't a lot to work with. You can forget dental charts and reconstruction of facial features without a skull. To make things worse we also lose eye color and hair style and color in case the head hair was dyed. I'm trying to make you understand that the results I did get are questionable in any court."

"I was at the scene," Lonto said, "there wasn't much to work with."

"Without limbs, even a man's weight and height are only estimates," Frienberg went on. "So I had to take some long shots."

"Such as?"

"I ran tests to determine if these men were poisoned or drugged before they were killed and came up with a dramatic reaction to cocaine in all three cases."

"Enough to kill them?"

"I don't think so," Frienberg said. "From the test results and condition of some of the remaining internal organs my guess is that all three of these men were long-term cocaine users."

"Addicts?"

"Or a pusher who had an unlimited source available. All three showed some damage to the inner lining of what remained of the windpipe. I would have liked to examine the nasal passages of these men, but of course that wasn't possible."

"Okay, we're dealing with three dead addicts or pushers then," Lonto said, "that cuts it down some."

"It was a start," Freinberg said, "but I used two more approaches. One of the men had been dead approximately three months, another we estimate between twenty and thirty days, and the last was relatively recent, between a week and ten days. We can't be exact because of the weather we're having. We asked Missing Persons for any reports on missing males in these time frames and the age groups our tests indicate."

"And?"

"We haven't heard from them yet," Isaac said. "But the most recent body also had a tattoo on his right upper chest . . . bear with me, Tony. Now, we've got a white male, blond, approximately thirty years old, six feet tall and one hundred and sixty pounds, and we know he's an addict and has type O blood. Plus we have an unusual tattoo, a horned angel seated astride the nipple of the right breast."

"Do we keep records of tattoos?" Lonto asked.

"Not of tattoos, but descriptions of them are listed on every felon that's arrested, just like scars are."

"You know how many felons there are in this city?" Lonto asked.

"That's where we might have gotten lucky," Isaac said, happily. "Hooley remembered the same tattoo listed on a felon he was matching fingerprints on. So we pulled the file and did some matching. Height, weight, age, color of hair, and blood type all match. The tattoo is listed on the man's prison file."

"Are you saying you can identify the body?"

"I'm saying there's a very strong likelihood it's the same man. But there's no dental work or fingerprints to match."

"Still . . ."

"And the blood type is common."

"How many blond men that age would have that tattoo?"

"That's what we think," Isaac said, pleased.

"Does this guy have a name?"

"My dad always told me to save the best part of the story for the last," Isaac said. "The man's name is Eddy Loyd."

"Oh," Lonto said, feeling let down.

"Somehow I don't detect overwelming enthusiasm in that 'Oh'," Isaac said.

"How long your man been dead?"

"Week to ten days."

"It won't fit," Lonto said. "Eddy Loyd left his fingerprints all over two murder scenes within the last week, one was two nights ago when your man was already in the morgue."

"Hmmm," Isaac said, "he might as well have signed his name.

"I thought maybe it had come together too easy," Isaac said. "Sorry about that."

"No problem. You guys have a good solid description of the man to work on."

"Now I think I spoiled my whole day," Isaac said, and hung up.

He had paid his apartment rent in advance for the two months he planned to be gone. Most of his packing was finished last night after he had put his car in storage. Everything was taken care of now, the money and cocaine were packed safely and with his police identification he didn't need to worry about any airport security searching his bags.

Last night he was sure someone had tried to break in and there were scratch marks on the lock, but they had left when he turned on the light. Had to be the one that had been following him. Good thing he was getting out of here today, out of Loyd's reach so he'd figure he had won. The slob wouldn't expect him to come back until he blew the back of Loyd's damn skull off some night. He planned his return right down to the details, even arranged to have some of the local junkies keep track of the drug action around. When he returned, he would take care of Loyd, check to see how many of the old customers were around, and use the police to eliminate any competition there might be. It had worked before, and he sure wasn't letting that scum-bag Loyd take away his action. He was almost tempted to stay in the city—forget moving south and use his buddies on the narcotics squad to make things hot for Loyd and his bunch of spics. Trouble was, if Loyd started to get too much pressure from them he just might give Pavolny's name to the Feds or something. He couldn't risk that. Well, he thought, no sense in taking unnecessary chances. He'd return, go back into business for a year, and then retire. Miami maybe. He'd have his retirement pay and a tax-free million or so to live on.

A cop was a fool if he didn't grab all the money he could when he was working. Fucking dealers made millions when *he* was taking home a few lousy hundred a week.

That crap wasn't for him.

He finished packing his toilet kit and carried it to the open suitcase on the couch. Looking down at the smaller suitcase he wondered how many cops had even had over a quarter million dollars. Not many. Work thirty years on the street and get retired on a pension you could starve on.

He closed the suitcase and stood looking around the apartment.

Took care of everything, he thought.

Catch a cab to the airport and have breakfast on the beach.

He was reaching for the suitcases when the door was kicked open. His first reaction was to reach for the gun clipped onto his belt. Then he saw Lonto and Runnion in the doorway and other men in the hall with their guns drawn.

"Don't even blink, Pavolny," Lonto said.

Pavolny didn't.

9

Nobody is happy when the cops bust a cop, except maybe the news services, delighted to have something to discuss on the five, ten, and late-night news, to say nothing about having news to splash across the evening and morning newspapers in screaming three-inch letters. DETECTIVE ARRESTED IN DRUG RAID! The following half page would explain that the city police needed a complete shake-up to stop the rapid spread of corruption.

Corruption did not appear to be rampant at the River Station. In the opinions of the detectives at shift change, busting a cop for a crime did not mean that all cops were on the take, even though city seemed to think so.

It was not a cheerful crew that morning. Even the announcement that the heat was now on in the building did not cheer them up.

Tony Lonto was in the lieutenant's office discussing yesterday's events with Jaworski, who was not known for his good humor even on the best of days.

"I don't know what the hell's the matter with cops nowadays," Jaworski said. "I'm just thankful as hell that Pavolny wasn't one of ours. We have enough problems as things are."

"Has he answered any questions yet?"

"He's making a deal on the advice of his attorney," Jaworski said. "What else can he do? We busted him with the money and two kilos of cocaine."

"What about his dealers?"

"He gave them up quick enough, Wells and Richards both

dead and, according to him, Eddy Loyd's the one who's killed them. A falling out among partners."

"We've been trying to find Loyd for a week," Lonto said, sourly.

"What about this cannibal thing?" Jaworski asked. "Right now, the commissioner is busy as a one-legged man at an ass-kicking contest but you can bet he's going to be on us to get that solved. He needs some positive press."

"We're coming up empty," Lonto said.

"You've got nothing?"

"There's no witnesses, no identification of the victims, and the crime took place in an area where no one lives. According to Ruiz these Caribes, or whoever they are, could live anywhere in the Latino quarter. Where do we start on this?"

"Where the hell *is* Ruiz anyway?"

"I didn't see him at all yesterday."

"Well, check with him," Jaworski said. "Maybe he's got some idea on where to find these people. He's the damn expert."

"That reminds me," Lonto said, "did you get any information from his record?"

"Yes, Captain Daniels looked at his file," Jaworski said. "He was a member of the secret police in Colombia for six years, a special group that was government controlled. That still doesn't connect him with the homicides O'Malley's working."

"No, it doesn't," Lonto said.

Jaworski sighed, and began tapping a pencil on his desk. "Alright, check it out if you have to, but keep it quiet. If you get anything positive turn it over to O'Malley and let him handle it. What I don't need is to ignore this and have another cop running around this city giving us a bad name."

"I'll check it out," Lonto said.

"And don't waste a lot of time on it. I want you working on this cannibal thing. Try some of our stoolies, somebody must know if a group like this has moved in."

"We'll get on it."

"Alright, get cracking. Does anyone use that stoolie, what the hell's his name? The one they call Pepi the Pimp?"

"I think Gonzalez works him."

"Then get him on him right away," Jaworski said. "And one more thing. I'll work out another set-up for our own light-fingered cop, but right now just stay on these murders. Goddamn whole police force is going to hell. All right, go on, Lonto, get moving."

"Right," Lonto said, and left the office.

Runnion, waiting for him in the squad room, handed Lonto a cup of bitter coffee and asked. "What's going on?"

"We need to put some time in on the Caribe homicides."

"Sure, all we need is a place to start," Runnion said. "Has the lab come up with any identification on the bodies?"

"They were waiting for a call from Missing Persons," Lonto said, picking up the phone. "Give Isaac a call and check, will you?"

Lonto made a call that morning to the Police Department in Miami. He identified himself as a detective, giving his badge number and department and asked to speak to the officer in charge of narcotics investigations in the Miami Beach district.

"What is this in regard to?" the police operator asked.

"A homicide investigation," Lonto said.

"Then you want Homicide."

"No. I want Narcotics," Lonto said, patiently.

"Oh, then this is a homicide investigation that involves narcotics?"

"Now you got it."

"That was the Miami Beach district?"

"Right."

"Just a minute."

Lonto waited.

"Narcotic Section, Captain Witley here," a deep voice said.

147

"Good morning. Captain, this is Detective Lonto . . ."

"Switchboard gave me all that," Witley cut in. "What's on you mind, Lonto?"

"I need some information on a case your section handled a while back involving drugs, and the possibility of cannibalism . . ."

"Just a minute," Witley said, and Lonto heard the phone being put down. A moment later, Witley came back on, "Okay, I forgot for a minute that Ruiz is up there in your fair city. How's he doing?"

"Still working on his pipeline last I heard," Lonto said.

"And still talking crazy about cannibals, I see," Witley said. "There wasn't any evidence that any cannibalism took place on that case, just some human blood and signs of a fire."

"Well, we've got some pretty conclusive evidence it happened here," Lonto said. "I wondered if you had any hard information on this group, these Caribes?"

"Hasn't Ruiz filled you in?"

"He's been very helpful," Lonto said. "What we need are names, descriptions, something to help us locate them."

"You guys really have a case of cannibalism?" Witley asked.

"It looks that way."

"We can't give you much as far as names and descriptions," Witley said. "We figure these people are in the country illegally. They don't have passports, ID's, social security numbers, or even birth certificates. The two that were killed during our operation were never identified. All we found on them was money and phony drivers' licenses."

"Not much to work with," Lonto said.

"We figure if it wasn't for the cocaine traffic we could have never gotten on to these people. We can send you what information we have, but it's not going to help you much."

"I'd appreciate it," Lonto said. "Seems like Detective Ruiz is our best source on this then."

Witley was silent for a long moment.

"Ruiz knows them alright," he said finally. "They're like an obsession with him sometimes. I figure he had some experience with them in Colombia. Gets a little crazy about them sometimes. But he's a good officer."

"He seems to know what he's doing," Lonto said. "One more thing, in your investigation did you have any homicides committed with a three-eighty?"

"One for sure," Witley said. "We can send you a ballistics report on the slug. Man was shot through the head at close range."

"Any others?"

"There was another homicide we figure was done by the same guy," Witley said. "In both cases the right ear was cut off but we were only able to recover one slug."

"Were they connected to the cocaine trade?" Lonto asked.

"We think so," Captain Witley said. "I'll send you copies of the investigation along with the rest. Let us know how your investigation works out."

"I will," Lonto said. "Thanks for your help."

Lieutenant Jaworski looked at the four detectives in his office, and then reached for one of his cigars:

"What the hell is going on around here anyway?" he muttered.

Lonto had filled O'Malley and Mills in on the information he had gotten on the .380 cartridge and Miami. In turn they had brought the lieutenant up to date on the two homicides O'Malley and Mills were investigating, and he had listened intently, his eyes shifting from one team to the other as they alternately picked up the threads of the investigation. The lieutenant looked tired. But there was a sense of deliberate authority about him: the knowledge that he had seen everything the streets had to offer before taking a desk job.

"Commissioner sends us this guy with orders to give him all the help he needs," Jaworski said. "What do they expect us to do? Ignore everything when it looks like he's some kind of vigilante on a goddamn vendetta."

"Well," Lonto said, "there's a possibility that this bunch he's after *could* be doing the killings."

"A damn slim possibility, from the looks of it. You say that type three-eighty cartridge is specially made for the police? Right?"

"That's right."

"And Ruiz was on a special narcotics task force down there," O'Malley said. "Those guys down there don't screw around."

"What about this ear thing?"

"I don't know if this fits in this case," Mills said. "But I heard, once, that on operation down there, when these special police raided a jungle cocaine factory, they would cut an ear off the dead dealers to prove their kills. They were paid a bounty or some damn thing. Something like the body counts we did in Nam."

"Did Ruiz ever say anything about these homicides?"

"He was only interested in the Wells and Richards killings."

"I thought we had Eddy Loyd tagged for those?"

"He is," Lonto said. "But he *could* be tied in with these people. Pavolny said Loyd had started working with South Americans. Maybe it's these Caribes."

"I hope they cook and eat that bastard," Jaworski muttered. "There were similar homicides in Miami, right?"

"Head shots, ear missing and a three-eighty," Lonto said. "I didn't ask too many questions about it but they promised to send us copies of the investigation."

"I just hate to charge an out-of-state officer," Jaworski shook his head. "The people he's after could be behind this, you know. But . . ."

The detectives waited in silence.

"Let's say we search Ruiz's place," Jaworski said. "And let's say we don't come up with anything. Then what?"

"Then this squad is in deep shit with the police commissioner and we won't be very popular with the Miami police either," Lonto said, helpfully.

"We're already in deep with the commissioner in case you haven't noticed," Jaworski said. "But suppose we don't move on this and Ruiz *is* our man? Then, we get our ass in a crack, no matter how many people will think he's doing the city a service killing people like that. Besides that, he's our best source of information on these people." He looked at Lonto. "You think all these homicides can be tied into one case?"

"They might all be connected to this Caribe group."

"What about you, O'Malley?"

"It all adds up," O'Malley said.

Jaworski thought about it while he lit his cigar, happily ignoring the looks of dismay on the detectives' faces.

"Okay. That's it then," he said finally. "Get a warrant, search his place and if we're wrong we'll take our lumps. I want both teams on this and be careful, the man's a cop. You get the warrant, O'Malley, it's your case. If we can catch him dirty maybe he will cooperate with Lonto on the other cases." He looked at the four men. "Anything else?"

They remained silent.

"Then get to it," Jaworski said. "And get me some results."

The desk clerk at the El Dorado had a hangover and was not pleased that his wife had thrown his bottle into the garbage; he wasn't overjoyed to see cops in the building either. He immediately informed O'Malley and Mills that if they wanted him to open any apartments in his building they could go back downtown and get a search warrant. O'Malley, who was prepared for exactly that, patiently presented him with the required document. The desk clerk said that the cops should spend more time searching other cops' apartments, according to what he read in the newspaper, and leave people who paid their rent alone.

The first thing O'Malley had asked the desk clerk was whether Ruiz was now in his apartment.

"He's out," the desk clerk said. "He went out about an hour ago. His key's in the box."

"Do you know where he went?"

"I don't keep track of the renters."

"Let's go look at his room," Mills said, "Lonto and Runnion will let us know if he comes back."

They began climbing. The stairwell was cool and clean despite the threadbare carpet and patches of peeled paint on the walls. The building smelled of wax and disinfectant, leading O'Malley to believe that the janitor in the building was a man serious about his work. The desk clerk kept complaining about his hangover all the way up to the fourth floor, telling O'Malley that most of the bars in the neighborhood made their whiskey from medical alcohol and tap water with a little food coloring and one of these days half the honest men around would go blind or die from poisoning and the cops would just ignore it like usual. He stopped outside a door with the numbers 42 on it, and handed O'Malley a key. Down the hall, they could hear a baby crying.

"Wish she'd feed that brat," the desk clerk said.

"Kids cry," O'Malley said, and unlocked the door.

"I'll be at the desk," the clerk said.

The room was small and clean. A double bed against the wall opposite the door. A lamp on the nightstand next to the bed. The faded blue curtains on the window had been pulled closed. Opposite the bed, there was a four-drawer dresser next to the closet door. On top of the dresser a shaving kit and folded towels. There was a small mirror fastened to the inside of the door next to a typed notice informing the resident that the hall bathroom was shared by all tenants on the floor.

"Looks like Ruiz traveled pretty light," Mills said.

"Let's get busy."

They made a quick check of the place, finding a skimpy wardrobe in the closet and two empty suitcases under the bed. There were towels and neatly folded underwear in the dresser. With the expertise of burglars, they started searching for a .380 caliber pistol or anything else that might tie Ruiz in to the homicides. They began the job at one-thirty. At three-thirty they were still looking.

They had made one trip downstairs for coffee and to check with Lonto and Runnion who were watching the entrance in case Ruiz returned. They had thoroughly searched the room and the bathroom down the hall, but had found nothing. They sat now on the stripped bed. The two lights in the room were on, casting a bright glare over the mess.

"Like I said, the man travels light."

Mills nodded in agreement. "Did you check the suitcases?"

"They're clean."

"There isn't any place to hide a gun," Mills said.

"Walls are solid," O'Malley said. "Anything we miss in the bathroom?"

"Nothing."

"You notice anything unusual about this place?"

"Like what?" Mills asked.

"A man on a long trip will usually take some personal things with him," O'Malley said. "There's nothing here, no letters, photos, keepsakes."

"Maybe anything personal he carries in his wallet," Mills said.

"Maybe."

"If you're in a strange city where would you hide a gun?" Mills asked. "Being a cop he sure knows where cops would look."

"I'd put it in a locker at the bus station," O'Malley said. "I'd want something a lot closer."

Mills looked at O'Malley and grinned.

"Has to be," O'Malley said. "I wouldn't leave nothing in a hotel room. Not when there's an all-night clerk and a big safe downstairs."

"Let's go," Mills said.

There was a heavy manila envelope with Ruiz's name on it in the hotel safe. Inside, four items. An envelope containing thirty-two hundred dollars in small bills. A four-by-six, framed photo of a black-haired man in a military uniform with a young boy standing beside him. The third item was a box of .380 caliber cartridges. Thirty cartridges remained in the fifty-round box. The final item puzzled the detectives for several minutes. It was a metal cylinder about two and a half inches in diameter; inside a thick cord on which oblong pieces of dried, leatherlike objects were strung.

"Looks like a string of dried mushrooms or something," O'Malley said, "packed in salt." He peered into the container, then held it under his nose to smell. "Doesn't smell much like anything I'd eat."

"Dump it," Mills said, "maybe there's something else."

They dumped the contents of the container on the empty manila envelope, spilling salt and the string of four objects. Two were obviously old and had dried into odd withered lumps. The remaining two objects were fresher and crusted with salt crystals.

O'Malley picked up the string and brushed the salt away. "Feels like rubber," he said. "What the hell?" He stared at the objects with widening eyes a long moment, then hastily dropped the string and began to wipe his fingers on his pants, swearing softly under his breath.

"What?" Mills asked, curiously.

"They're *ears*," O'Malley said. "He's keeping score."

Mills stepped back from the desk as though the string had just turned into a snake. O'Malley continued wiping his hands.

Victor Ruiz had bought four packages of cocaine from a pusher on Rice Street about two-thirty in the afternoon. He was wearing jeans once more and knew from his previous visits on Rice Street that the park was the place to find the addicts in the area. By five o'clock that evening the four small packages of cocaine were gone and the grateful addicts had helpfully pointed out three pushers who had been working the park that day.

Ruiz had followed the pusher the addicts had called Paco when he left the park at dusk, knowing he would make his rounds of the bars and eventually return to the building where the other Caribes lived. He was not interested in the building now. It was too dangerous for him to return there after killing the first man. He had risked it once so they would know he had found them again. He *would* risk it again. He shivered slightly, thinking what they would do to him if they caught him. For now, he would be content to find their men, one at a time.

On two occasions during the next hour the pusher left the crowded sidewalks on Rice Street and made stops at the apartment buildings along the side streets. Ruiz knew he was moving steadily toward his own apartment building. Smiling, Ruiz considered the place he would kill him, a dark street within a block of where he would be safe. Once tonight he thought the pusher had recognized him. He had followed the man too quickly into a bar only to find the man looking directly at him when he pushed open the door. But the pusher had turned away and spoke into a pay phone on the wall for ten minutes before he returned to the street.

When the pusher left the bar Ruiz stayed a safe distance behind him, wondering why this one was so careless. Not once since he had left the park had the man checked to see if he was being tailed. It was almost like the man was making it easy for him or that they did not consider him a threat to them. But that couldn't be; he had hunted them in his country and in Miami, and now he had found them here. They knew he would not stop. Although they considered the police to be stupid and viewed those that were not Caribe with disdain, he knew they considered *him* a very real threat to them, just as his father had always been.

They knew he would kill them without hesitation, like the animals they were. He was not hampered by the human laws that would protect them. They only understand an enemy who killed as they killed.

The pusher reached the corner of Eighty-second Street and paused a moment. The sidewalks were less crowded here and Ruiz considered crossing the street to follow him from the other side. He stopped to look in a small shop window when the pusher approached a girl standing at the curb a half block away. From the corner of his eye he could see they were arguing. The pusher grabbed the girl by the arm and pawed at her breasts.

The girl slapped him and fought silently as the pusher tore her blouse. Without thinking Ruiz began running toward them. When the pusher pulled a knife from his jacket it was Ruiz's first thought to protect the girl from a thing he hated, even if he lost the opportunity to kill the man. As he ran, he saw the girl break free and run towards him, the pusher following for a short distance before turning into an alley just as the girl reached Ruiz and threw her arms around him.

"You're safe," Ruiz said, putting his arms around the girl and watching the alley.

He realized that one of the girl's hands was tightly clamped over the gun clipped onto his belt under the shirt, and tried to push her away, knowing as he did that he was too late. He was staring directly into her dark Caribe eyes as she drove the knife in under his ribs and twisted it savagely.

"Pig," she whispered, and spit at his face as he fell forward. In the distance he could hear the sound of a police siren and the sound of the girl running. He thought about his father sadly, and began to pray softly wondering if the police would get a priest in time.

Lonto and Runnion arrived at the scene before the ambulance.

Two patrolmen knelt beside Ruiz, unsure of what to do about the blood soaking his shirt and jacket. Ruiz was still alive but he had taken the knife at an upward angle just under the ribs near the center of his chest. He was spitting blood, and mumbling to himself.

Lonto swore softly as he knelt beside him.

"Ruiz," Lonto said. "This is Lonto, who did this?"

"Is there a priest?" Ruiz asked.

"We'll get you one at the hospital."

Ruiz opened his eyes and smiled.

"Who was it?" Lonto asked. "Who stabbed you?"

"Girl," Ruiz said, "Caribe girl."

"Do you know where the Caribes are?"

Ruiz gripped his arm weakly. "You must kill them," he said, "all of them or it will go on."

"We'll get them," Lonto said. "Where can we find them?"

Ruiz mumbled in Spanish.

"Where, Ruiz?"

"Galeas, seven . . . ah . . . ah," he said, and died as O'Malley and Mills pulled up.

He was trying to say 703 Rice Street.

They found a notebook in his back pocket, the notes of his daily investigations. In it was the name Anthony Galeas and the address 703 Rice Street.

"That's the name of the first homicide victim," O'Malley said, taking out his notebook. "Anthony Galeas, father's name's Tino, and the sister who found the body was called Arcadia, right address, too."

"Ruiz said they're the people we're looking for," Lonto said, "these Caribes or whatever the hell they are."

O'Malley and Mills exchanged glances.

"If they are Caribes it's going to take more than the four of us to make an arrest," O'Malley said. "There's around thirty people in that building, most of them men."

"Galeas. That's what Ruiz said?"

"Just the girl, and the old man who looked about a hundred years old. The girl said he was her father," Mills said. "Come to think about it, everyone in that building seemed to know each other. Usually a guy don't know who the guy in the next apartment is."

"Big apartment building?" Runnion asked.

"Only three floors, buildings beside it and in back were deserted," O'Malley said. "There's a coffee shop and grocery on the first floor, rooms on the other two."

"Anyone get a description of the girl who knifed him?" Lonto asked.

"Patrolmen only saw her running," Runnion said, "before she went into the alley there. Young, dark skin, black-haired."

The men grew silent as the ambulance pulled up. Later, watching the body being loaded in the ambulance, Lonto said, "We better move on this."

They scheduled the raid on 703 Rice Street for ten o'clock that night, after Jaworski decided that it would take at least that long to put together a team large enough to handle the job. In theory, the ideal formula for a raid: surprise plus overwhelming strength equals success (no dead cops). It was a very good theory when kicking in apartment doors or arresting a suspect in some flophouse. It was a bit more hairy when you wanted to arrest someone in a building where you knew there were thirty or more people who each had some very good reasons not to get arrested. It is difficult to move enough men into the area and maintain the element of surprise, especially in a neighborhood where the citizens can spot a cop six blocks away.

The ideal formula was shot to hell when they learned that only sixteen men were available for the raid without stripping the rest of the precinct of police protection.

Jaworski's phone call to the police commissioner brought the added cheerful news that neither of the city's two SWAT teams were available; one was occupied trying to talk a drunk with a gun out of a car downtown and the other was patiently waiting for an armed robber to leave the jewelry store he had been trapped in. Jaworski wished they had more men available.

The rest of the homicide squad wished they had a tank or at least a hundred or so Rambo-type marines. After discussing the half-eaten bodies found at the construction site they decided that maybe two hundred Rambo-type marines were needed. The six detectives who were to lead the team also decided they would carry three of the twelve gauge riot guns available in the arms room since a load of buckshot is a sure cure for anyone intent on chopping your head off.

An additional problem developed over who would lead the assembled team. While O'Malley and Mills had first investigated the Galeas homicide and could identify both the suspects, Lonto and Runnion were the investigation officers on the other homicides—in Lonto's opinion Eddy Loyd might also be found with the Caribes.

Lieutenant Jaworski, with the wisdom of Solomon, solved the problem by stating flatly that Vincent Gonzalez would lead the raid since he was the only man available who spoke Spanish and he didn't want anyone killed over a misunderstanding.

There were six detectives and ten patrolmen working the raid. From the building's layout as O'Malley and Mills remembered it, they would work in two teams. The first team, consisting of four detectives and six patrolmen, led by Gonzalez, would go through the grocery store and up the stairs to the apartment where the suspects lived. The second team, consisting of Lonto and Runnion, along with four patrolmen, would secure the grocery store and café combination and cover the back stairway which led down into the café. The outside of the building would be secured by the men in the patrol cars that would be called into the area.

They all agreed it was as good a plan as could be expected considering the circumstances. No one mentioned that even the best-laid plans had a way of becoming rapidly unraveled.

The two unmarked sedans, followed by the two police

vans packed with the ten patrolmen, who were afraid the detectives would certainly get them killed, pulled up directly in front of 703. The moment the cars stopped the men piled out gratefully and moved swiftly toward the door of the grocery, guns drawn. Vincent Gonzalez in the lead, shouted in Spanish as soon as they hit the door. The first team went up the stairs quickly leaving Lonto and Runnion with the other patrolmen to secure the small grocery store and café. Both were empty. Lonto stationed a patrolman at each staircase, and, with Runnion and the shotgun as back up, moved to check the rooms on the left side of the café.

Upstairs, they could hear Gonzalez shouting and the sound of a door being kicked open.

The first door Lonto reached opened into an empty storeroom. Runnion went in past Lonto to throw open the door into a small toilet, also empty. Lonto and Runnion exchanged glances, wondering if they again had successfully raided an empty building. Lonto nodded toward the door under the back staircase and both men moved across the room to flank it. Holding the shotgun in one hand, Runnion reached down to turn the knob. The door swung open and they saw a dimly lit stairway leading into the basement.

"Wait until we clear the rest of the building," Lonto said.

Upstairs, they could hear Gonzalez still shouting and the sound of men running. The two patrolmen backing up Lonto and Runnion exchanged glances and grinned at each other. If there was nobody home it was fine with them.

"Let's check that," Lonto said, going toward the door in the back of the café. The door was hung to open into the café, which forced both detectives to stand on the lock side. The system Lonto and Runnion had developed over the years was to open the door and take a quick look inside, hopefully before someone shot your head off, deciding how to enter after the door was open. Neither of them liked the idea of entering the room from the same side.

Lonto dropped to his knees, pulled the door open and looked quickly around the corner as the door was swinging back. He sat there blinking, unsure of what he had just seen.

"What?" Runnion asked.

"Take a look."

Runnion leaned forward and glanced quickly around the corner.

The courtyard between the buildings was dark except for the small fire that clearly lighted the man seated behind it.

"What do you think?" Lonto asked.

"There could be a thousand of them out there," Runnion said.

"Yeah," Lonto said, watching the two patrolmen move up.

Runnion nodded to the patrolmen, "Cover us," he said.

Lonto rose. "I'll take the right," he said and leaped through the door, expecting the darkness to brighten up with gun flashes. He could hear Runnion moving behind him.

Nothing happened.

Flattened to the building on either side of the door they faced the man at the fire. In the flickering light he remained motionless. He was naked from the waist up, wearing only a red headband over his white, shoulder-length hair. He sat cross legged, hands folded over a long object in his lap, and watched them silently. Only the fire moved light across his deeply wrinkled face.

"Police!" Runnion shouted. "Put your hands on your head and don't move!"

The man remained motionless, watching them with bright eyes.

To a cop, two policemen pointing guns at you were two very good reasons to follow instructions, hastily. The motionless man made them hesitate and they didn't want to go forward without knowing what was waiting in the dark. They kept pressed against the building.

"Think he understands English?" Runnion asked.

Lonto watched the man intently, feeling a growing

tenseness. "Get Gonzalez," he said to the patrolmen at the door.

"I understand you," the man said. He stood up slowly. He stood quietly facing them holding a long corn knife in his right hand.

"Drop the knife," Runnion said, loudly.

The man spit into the fire.

"What's your name?" Lonto asked, feeling uneasy, though the man was fifteen feet away.

"I am Galeas here," the man said.

"Where's your daughter," Lonto asked, wanting to keep him talking. "Where's the rest of your people?"

"They are beyond your reach," Galeas said. "She leads them now."

"They left you here?"

The man remained silent, watching.

"Why don't you put down . . ." Lonto began.

The man screamed suddenly and leaped over the fire directly at Lonto with the long knife raised. It was a deep, primeval scream filled with hate that froze the cops and raised the hair on the backs of their necks. One of the patrolmen in the doorway fired blindly into the building across the courtyard and ducked back into the room.

The sound of the shot broke Lonto from the grip of surprise and he fired. The first slug seemed to have no effect and Lonto fired again, unconsciously trying to back away from the screaming charge. The second slug had no more effect than the first and Lonto raised his arms against the knife when the heavy roar of the shotgun slammed on his left. The buckshot charge knocked the man off his feet. He twisted on the stone courtyard, attempted to rise, coughed blood, and then collapsed on his face.

The silence in the courtyard seemed to ring in their ears. They watched the darkness beyond the fire.

Nothing moved but shadows from the fire.

Lonto shivered.

"Jesus fucking Christ," Runnion said.

They approached the body cautiously, Lonto kicking the corn knife away from the outstretched arm. He hated knives of any kind having once been cut by a twelve-year-old, high on angel dust. In death, the man seemed shrunken and ancient, but both men would always see him as he had looked leaping over the fire. He had appeared at least eight feet tall!

Lonto stared silently at the man. He couldn't stop shivering.

"What the hell's he wearing on his hands?" Runnion asked. "I never seen gloves like that before."

Lonto was not interested in gloves. He was only interested in going home to Robin and holding her until he could stop shivering. "Let's finish up and get the hell out of here or we won't get home until noon tomorrow."

10

Nobody likes cases that have too many loose ends. Lieutenant Jaworski especially did not like cases with loose ends, which would likely remain in the open file until the files were forgotten. In truth, none of the detectives on the squad were pleased about open cases because they reminded them that someone had gotten away with murder. They had issued an arrest warrant for Arcadia Galeas, though they knew that was probably not her name. The police laboratory had worked far into the wee hours of the morning examining the building and carefully lifting hundreds of fingerprints from the rooms that were now empty.

The raid had netted them only the old man known as Tino Galeas. The rest of the Caribes were gone, as was Eddy Loyd; if in fact he had ever been with the group. Everyone on the squad was aware that the Police Commissioner would not be pleased to know that the Caribes had packed up their cocaine and corn knives and were now free to begin operations again in this or some other city. The detectives unanimously hoped they had picked some other city. No one was surprised to learn that Lieutenant Jaworski had called a squad meeting that morning.

"After last night I know this isn't the best squad in the damn city," Jaworski began, eyeing them, "and we'll get to that later. Right now, we have another problem to deal with."

They waited silently.

"Last night there was a lot of traffic around here with

everyone bringing some damn thing or other into the property room." He looked around the room from face to face before he went on. "And sometime last night someone decided to take a few things out of the evidence room while they were in there."

"What are you saying . . ." Runnion began.

"Just shut up!" Jaworski barked. "Last night someone opened one of the evidence bags and lifted two ounces of cocaine."

Every man in the room looked uneasily around at the other.

"It's not the first time it's happened," Jaworski said, "but this time he's not getting away with it. Has anyone got anything to say?"

He waited as the silence grew in the room.

"Okay then," he said, "pull those drapes shut over the window." He waited as Gonzalez closed the drapes. "Now everyone stay exactly where they are, and you turn off the lights, O'Malley."

"What the hell," someone mumbled in the darkened room as Jaworski turned on the lamp on his desk, casting an eerie light in the room.

"It's black light," Jaworski said. "It reacts to a powder the lab provided, the same powder that was on the cocaine taken from the evidence room last night."

Jaworski was silent, knowing he didn't have to say any more. All eyes were on the brightly glowing hands of someone by the bookcase. Fascinated, they watched as the hands seemed to move by themselves, hanging in the air before vanishing into the dark.

"Lights," Jaworski said.

They blinked as the lights came on. Runnion and Mills stepped away from the bookcase leaving David Washington standing alone with his hands in his pockets, his teeth clenched as though he were in pain. He faced the rest of the squad.

"I can explain . . ." he began.

"First, I want your gun and shield," Jaworski said, flatly.

Lonto watched him walk to the desk and lay his gun and shield in front of the lieutenant. Runnion looked away as the other detectives avoided looking at each other and shuffled their feet uneasily.

"The rest of you get out of here," Jaworski said, picking up the phone.

At his desk, Lonto glanced over at Runnion who was talking softly on the phone. He felt guilty about not being sure of Pat, and realized that Jaworski hadn't been completely sure of any of the squad either. He rubbed his face sleepily and sighed as the phone rang.

Detective Isaac Frienberg was delighted with himself that morning. He was even beginning to think that his assistant Hooley was becoming one hell of a medical examiner under his training. He had once considered Hooley a bumbling idiot who didn't know a scapel from a potato peeler. After checking Hooley's report and running some tests of his own, he was in high spirits when he called Lonto.

"River Station, Lonto."

"Morning," Isaac said. "How's everything at the famed River Station today? I hear you guys were busy last night solving homicides."

"Without much success," Lonto said, sourly.

"You might have done better than you think," Isaac said. "This Tino Galeas they brought in last night, I understand he was involved with the cannibalism case."

"He's the only one we can tie into it," Lonto said. "The rest were gone when we got there."

"This is the same bunch Eddy Loyd was involved with, right?" Isaac asked.

"We think so," Lonto said. "We didn't find him on the raid, either."

"In a way, you did find him," Isaac said, "and I still think we've got his body here in the morgue."

"I'm too tired for this, Isaac," Lonto said. "I thought we already decided that the man you have there was dead be-

166

fore Loyd started chopping up pushers with his new friends. Don't tell me the lab screwed up?"

"No, our estimated time of death is as close as we can get," Isaac said. "But remember that everything else matched? Blood type, height, weight, right down to the tattoo?"

"Right," Lonto said, "and the body was already in the morgue when Loyd killed the pusher. So where does that leave us?"

"How do you know Loyd did those killings?" Isaac asked.

"In one case he left his fingerprints all over the murder weapon, and in the other his prints were all over the apartment we searched after the murder," Lonto said. "Hell, Isaac, you know all this. Your boys ran the lab work."

"Pretty careless of him, wasn't it," Isaac asked, "leaving his prints around to make it easy for us?"

"He already knew we were looking for him," Lonto said. "He left his own apartment looking like a butcher shop."

"But the only thing we have is his fingerprints, right?"

"Right. So?"

"Okay," Isaac said. "Now, remember this summer when you were working that floater case, the body was too decomposed to get prints like we normally would."

"I remember you identified the guy."

"Right, but we had to take the skin off the fingers, and print it by wearing the skin over one of our gloves. Hell of a mess," Isaac said, "but it worked."

"What's this have to do with Eddy Loyd?"

"A lot," Isaac said. "This is what we were able to put together." He cleared his throat. "This Tino Galeas, who was brought in last night, was wearing some sort of gloves. Hooley examined them and called me and we ran some more tests. What these gloves were was the skin from a man's hand, peeled off much like you would take a pair of real gloves off. From the tests, we know they probably soaked the skin in some ashes and salt solution and then used smoke to dry them. They actually tanned the skin like people once tanned leather. We had Hooley wear them and printed him. Wearing these things like gloves he left a perfect set of Eddy Loyd's prints."

Lonto was silent.

"You still there?" Isaac asked, finally.

"What you're saying is that Loyd has been dead for more than a week," Lonto said, "and they were using his hands?"

"The skin from his hands," Isaac corrected. "We ran tests on the skin and on the body in the morgue. It's Eddy Loyd alright. Anyone could wear those things and leave Loyd's prints."

Lonto sighed.

"You should stop over and take a look at these things," Isaac said, "it's surprising how they did it."

"Some other time," Lonto said. "It explains why we couldn't find Loyd, and leaves us with the Caribes as the suspects. At least we know who was murdered in Eddy Loyd's apartment. *That's* where he was killed."

"One thing bothers me," Isaac said.

"What's that?"

"Why did they leave these things with the old man? We would have just kept looking for Loyd."

Lonto looked out the window at the city. "I don't know why these people do *anything*," he said. "Maybe they don't care if we know how they did it because we don't know whose hands they might use next time. There's a few million people to choose from out there."

"I'm just glad we finally identified at least one of these bodies," Isaac said. "I knew that *had* to be Loyd with that tattoo. It was the fingerprints that fooled me."

"They fooled us all, Isaac," Lonto said. "Thanks for your help."

Hanging the phone up, he shook his head and turned to see Runnion grinning at him.

"What's up?" Runnion asked.

Lonto told him.

When he was finished, Runnion said, "I'll be damned,"

and kept grinning like he'd just won the lottery or something.

"What the hell are you grinning about?" Lonto asked, and smiled himself.

"I just talked to the hospital," he said, happily. "They found a donor for Lin. The operation's this afternoon, soon as the plane gets here."

"That's great," Lonto said. "What the hell you still doing here?"

"Waiting for you," Runnion said. "We can pick up Robin and go out together, if you guys want to. We've got the rest of the day off anyway."

"We'll be there," Lonto said, "soon as I give Jaworski the news from Isaac."

Outside, they were met by dark clouds and a cold north wind that drove sleet into their face. The clear fall days had slipped away, leaving the threat of winter hanging over the city.

Lonto thought about Eddy Loyd and the Caribes briefly, then he pushed the thoughts from his mind and walked with the grinning Runnion towards the parking lot.